"Maybe this parenting thing isn't so hard."

Cara laughed. "Yeah, you keep thinking that, Noah."

"I believe my new housekeeper is making fun of me."

Arching an eyebrow, Cara asked, "You think?"

Amusement dimpled Noah's cheeks. "I bow before your expertise in child rearing. Believe me, I'm in over my head and still wondering why I agreed to take in three kids."

"Because you saw a need and wanted to help."

"So you think you've got me figured out," Noah said.

"No, I would never say that." Cara blushed. "Now I need to get busy cleaning. If you stay, I'll put you to work."

"I'm all yours till I have to pick up the kids from school."

I'm all yours. Cara couldn't get past those words. But she had to remember that Noah was a self-proclaimed bachelor for life. And all she wanted was a family. She shouldn't have taken this job. Noah wasn't going to be an easy man to ignore.

Books by Margaret Daley

Love Inspired

The Power of Love #168
Family for Keeps #183
Sadie's Hero #191
The Courage To Dream #205
What the Heart Knows #236
A Family for Tory #245
**Gold in the Fire* #273
**A Mother for Cindy* #283
**Light in the Storm* #297
The Cinderella Plan #320
**When Dreams Come True* #339
**Tidings of Joy* #369
***Once Upon a Family* #393
***Heart of the Family* #425
***Family Ever After* #444

*The Ladies of Sweetwater Lake
**Fostered by Love

Love Inspired Suspense

Hearts on the Line #23
Heart of the Amazon #37
So Dark the Night #43
Vanished #51
Buried Secrets #72
Don't Look Back #92

MARGARET DALEY

feels she has been blessed. She has been married more than thirty years to her husband, Mike, whom she met in college. He is a terrific support and her best friend. They have one son, Shaun.

Margaret has been writing for many years and loves to tell a story. When she was a little girl, she would play with her dolls and make up stories about their lives. Now she writes these stories down. She especially enjoys weaving stories about families and how faith in God can sustain a person when things get tough. When she isn't writing, she is fortunate to be a teacher for students with special needs. Margaret has taught for over twenty years and loves working with her students. She has also been a Special Olympics coach and has participated in many sports with her students.

Family Ever After

Margaret Daley

Published by Steeple Hill Books™

STEEPLE HILL BOOKS

ISBN-13: 978-0-373-87480-4
ISBN-10: 0-373-87480-4

FAMILY EVER AFTER

This edition published by arrangement with Steeple Hill Books.

www.SteepleHill.com

Printed in U.S.A.

But the salvation of the righteous is of the Lord:
he is their strength in the time of trouble.
—*Psalms* 37:39

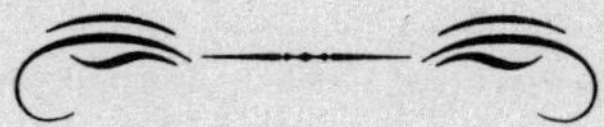

To my new granddaughter
I love you.

Chapter One

A clap of thunder vibrated the air. Cara Winters jumped at the sudden sound. Staring out the windshield of her blue Chevy, she could barely see the front door of the restaurant ten yards away. Sheets of gray rain hammered the packed parking lot. With a glance at the clock, noting it was twenty minutes after noon, she grabbed her umbrella from the seat next to her.

She hated being late. Again she studied the distance to the restaurant and noted a lessening in the intensity of the storm. If she hurried, she shouldn't get too wet.

Clasping the handle, she readied herself for the mad dash. She shot out of the car, opening the umbrella as she slammed the door closed with her foot. Then she rushed toward The Ultimate Pizzeria, her total attention on the entrance.

Halfway across the parking lot, a blaring horn froze her. She pivoted toward the noise, her eyes growing round. A red sports car swerved to avoid her and splashed a puddle of water down her front. The wind caught on her umbrella, and turned it inside out. What the puddle of water didn't get wet, the pouring rain did.

She sidestepped another small lake and continued her sprint to the restaurant. Maybe they had a towel—or several—she could use. Being drenched was a fitting end to her horrible morning.

As she reached to open the door, out of the corner of her eye she noticed the red sports car park in the back. She thought about waiting to give the driver a piece of her mind, but that would take time and energy she didn't have.

Shivering from being cold and wet, she welcomed the warmth in the pizzeria as she scanned the tables for her son and Laura Stone. Her friend waved from the other side of the restaurant, and Cara quickly made her way to the table beside one of the large picture windows that faced the street.

"I'm sorry I'm late. The second interview ran over, but I didn't get the job. Either one." Cara slipped into the chair across from Laura and smiled at Timothy, whose mouth was full of a bread stick.

Her friend's gaze widened. "I'm sorry about the jobs, but what happened to you? Did you go swimming? I know you're new to town, but it's only March and still cold in Cimarron City."

"Funny. I'm laughing on the inside."

"Seriously, what happened?" Laura dumped a packet of sugar into her iced tea and stirred it.

"I almost got run over in the parking lot, and the guy didn't even bother to check and see if I was all right. What has happened to chivalry in this century?"

Timothy swallowed his food. "What's chiv-alry?"

"Hon, it's about courage, honor and protecting the weak."

"You aren't weak, Mom."

Cara chuckled. "No, but I am wet."

She noticed her friend's gaze shift to something behind Cara. Before she had a chance to peer over her shoulder to see what had captured Laura's attention, a thick terry cloth towel was dropped onto the table in front of her. She must really look bad if a stranger was giving her something to dry off with.

Cara twisted around in her chair to thank her rescuer. A tall, lean man with shaggy dark brown hair filled her vision. Her gaze traveled up his torso and came to light on the somber expression of the man who had nearly hit her. All words fled from her mind as she stared into his hazel eyes.

"Noah, when did you arrive? When I came in, they said you had a business meeting and had gone to your office."

Cara heard her friend speaking to the man, but she couldn't tear her gaze away. From the distance in the parking lot and the heavy rain, she hadn't really gotten a good, up-close look at him. Now she did, and he was probably the handsomest man she'd ever seen. Bar none!

Averting his gaze from her, Noah grinned at Timothy and then Laura as he sat in an empty chair. "I just got here. I see you're with the woman I nearly ran down." He gave Cara an apologetic look, the corners of his mouth curving up while dimples appeared in his cheeks. "I'm very sorry. I didn't see you between the parked cars. I would have stopped, but I didn't want you to get wetter than you already were."

Heat seared her face. She lowered her gaze and fastened it upon the towel. "Thanks for this." She lifted it and wiped her damp hair and face.

"This is my friend Cara Winters, and her son, Timothy, from St. Louis. She finally decided to take me up on my suggestion to move here."

After greeting her son, the man held his hand out for Cara to shake. "Nice to meet you. I'm Noah Maxwell, the proprietor of this fine establishment. I know my armor is a bit tarnished, but I hope the towel and apology restore some faith in chivalry."

Timothy giggled.

She paused in an attempt to make herself more presentable and draped the towel over the arm of the chair. She clasped his hand and shook it once before releasing it. Her fingers tingled from the warmth radiating from his hand. "You're a friend of Laura's husband, aren't you?"

"Yeah, we've known each other for years. Peter, Jacob and I were foster brothers."

"Ah, yes. I met Jacob and his wife yesterday."

"How long have you been here?"

"Just a few days."

Noah transferred his attention to Laura. "Why didn't you say your friend was moving here? I know how long you've been wanting her to come."

Cara folded her hands in her lap—tightly—to erase the warmth of his fingers about hers a moment ago, but she still felt the touch. "Not her fault. She didn't know until the last minute. I finally sold my house and had been planning to move into an apartment in St. Louis." She glanced at her son. "Both Timothy and I decided since we had to move why not come to Oklahoma. He missed Laura's boys. They were buddies. And I missed Laura."

"Cara is a free spirit. When I asked her to come to Cimarron City, I extended an open-ended invitation, which I'm thrilled she accepted. I'd about given up on her moving here." Laura leaned forward. "We want to keep her here, so she needs a job and a place to stay. Any suggestions?"

Noah scanned his restaurant. "Have you ever been a waitress? One of mine will be going on maternity leave at the end of this week."

Cara shook her head. Like Laura, she had been a wife, mother and homemaker with no skills beyond that. Not very marketable, she'd realized after the fifth interview with no hope of a job. "Unless you count waiting on my family at mealtime."

"Close enough. You're hired."

Her mouth fell open. "Just like that?" She snapped her fingers and her lips closed.

Noah's laughter spiced the air. "I need a temporary waitress. You need a job."

"Don't you have to check my references?" Despite her lack of experience in the workforce, even she knew that much.

Noah turned to Laura. "Will you vouch for your friend?"

"One hundred percent. You won't get a better worker than her."

Noah then shifted his attention to Timothy. "What do you say about your mom? Is she a good worker?"

"She's the best!" Timothy scooped up another bread stick and took a bite.

Noah's sharp, assessing gaze swiveled back to Cara. "There. I've checked your references. Do you want the job? I know it probably isn't what you're looking for, but it's temporary until my waitress comes back in six weeks. The tips aren't bad here, and it'll give you some time to look for a different job."

Two warm patches continued to flame her cheeks. She wasn't used to a man looking at her with such intensity. Married right out of high school, she'd basically led a sheltered life where men were involved. "As long as you know I've never done anything like this."

Noah rose. "I'm a risk taker. I think I can handle it. Can you start on Friday? The weekends are very busy around here. You might as well plunge right in."

Three days. "Sure." Thoughts flew through her mind. She had so much to do before she started the job. Enroll her son in school. Start looking for a place to live. She didn't want to live off Laura's—or anyone's—charity for long.

"I'll see you at eleven then on Friday."

The quick smile that graced his mouth made Cara's heart palpitate. After he left, she said, "Once I get past the fact he almost ran me down with his car, he's a charmer."

"Noah is a dear friend. He's very charming and kind, but he's left a string of broken hearts in Cimarron City," Laura said.

Cara straightened, lining up her fork and knife next to her plate. "You don't need to worry about me."

"Mom, I need to go to the bathroom."

Cara began to rise.

"I'm eight. I can go by myself."

"Sure, hon. You see where it is?"

He nodded and left.

When he disappeared inside the restroom, Cara swung back to her friend. "Just because I said Noah Maxwell was charming, doesn't mean I'm interested, Laura. Being married once was enough for me. My son and I are happy the way things are." If she said it enough, surely she would begin to believe it.

"It seems the last year I was in St. Louis all we talked about were my problems. You haven't talked much about your marriage to Tim."

Although the sentence wasn't really a query, Cara glimpsed the question in her friend's eyes. "It's not a secret we were talking about divorcing before he became sick. I couldn't leave him when that happened. I'm not even sure I could have if he'd remained healthy." Her husband's long illness had wiped out their savings and what little life insurance he had went to finish paying off his medical bills and to give her some time to figure out what to do with her life. But she still didn't know what that was.

A waitress brought a large Canadian bacon pizza and placed it in the middle of the table. After she left with Cara's drink order, Laura said, "I took the liberty of ordering. Timothy seemed to think you wouldn't mind."

The aroma wafting to Cara made her mouth water. "Not one bit. I'm starved. I got out of your house this morning so fast I didn't even get a cup of coffee. Thankfully I didn't yawn through the interviews."

"Noah's pizzas are fabulous even if I'm a little partial."

Cara surveyed the busy restaurant, noticing Timothy weaving his way back to them. "It's a good thing I like pizza since I'll be working here at least for the time being. Now all I have to do is find a place to live with my son."

"You've got one for the time being. My house."

"I can't impose for long. You already have too many people under one roof."

"The more the merrier, I say. Remember I chose to have four children, so I'm accustomed to a lot of people around." Laura grinned. "Besides, soon our new addition will be finished and we'll have two more bedrooms."

"No, this is important. I have to make it on my own. I hope you understand." She couldn't make the same mistake again of depending on someone else to rescue her.

Laura fixed her with a kind look. "I understand perfectly. You remind me of myself this time two years ago when I first came to Cimarron City." She took a slice of pizza. "But remember you aren't alone. The Lord is with you and so are your friends."

If only it were that simple. Cara picked up her own piece to eat while Timothy reseated himself. Her son had to be her main focus now.

Two days later, Cara stretched as far as she could on the second to the top rung of an eight-foot ladder, leaning against the trunk of an oak. "Kitty. Here, kitty. You've got to take this. You won't get well if you don't take it." Although, by the way this tomcat scampered up the tree, it appeared as though he was healthier than everyone thought.

Cara held a treat between her forefinger and thumb and waved it toward him. The overweight cat, sitting on the branch above her, let out a protesting whine. Obviously this feline was too smart to fall for the hidden pill inside the moist delicacy.

She glanced at the top rung and decided there was no way she would go that extra step for the tomcat. She was high enough off the ground as it was. When she looked back at the animal, entrenched in his safe spot, the cat launched himself at her. She flung up her arm to protect her face. The action caused the ladder to rock back. For a second it teetered in midair, and then suddenly Cara plunged toward the hard ground.

Masculine arms caged her against the wooden rungs but the ladder's backward momentum was too much. She continued to fall, taking her rescuer with her. His body cushioned her impact. A grunt exploded from his lips, blasting hot air near her ear; at the same time, muddy water splashed up, drenching her and the person under her.

One of the slats hit her forehead as the traitorous ladder came to rest on top of her and her mysterious protector.

"Okay?"

The deep timbre of his voice washed over her much like the puddle. She gripped the ladder and shoved it off her, embarrassment making her unusually strong, it seemed.

"Yes. How about you?"

He lifted her up a few inches and sucked in several deep breaths. "Now I am."

She scrambled to the side and rotated toward her rescuer. The color in her cheeks had to have deepened to a scarlet red, if the warmth suffusing her face was any indication, and she was glad that the muddy water covered her mortification.

"I guess you attract puddles," Noah said as he scooted back out of the muddy water, which drenched both of them now.

She pushed her wet hair back from her face and wiped her hands across her cheeks. "One of my finer abilities."

His chuckles echoed through Laura's backyard. "I'm not sure I want to know about any others." He rose in one smooth motion and presented his hand to help her stand.

On her feet she saw how totally soaked she was. Far worse than a few days ago when she had first met Noah Maxwell. "I don't think a towel will help this time."

He glanced down his body. "You think?" When he reestablished eye contact with her, amusement glittered in his hazel depths. "Where is everyone?"

"Peter is at the barn. Laura and the children are at the cottages, making plans for tomorrow."

"Tomorrow?"

"The last day of freedom, as Laura's son told me, before they have to go back to school."

Puzzlement wrinkled his brow.

"Last day of spring break and the first day of my new job."

"Ah, I see. I would think Sean would be looking forward to going back. He only has a few more months and he will graduate."

"Top of his class as Laura is eager to point out."

"Yeah, he's come a long way from two years ago."

"A lot can happen in two years." As she well knew. Her life had fallen apart and everything familiar was gone. "Can I help you?"

"Why were you on the ladder?"

Cara glanced up into the branches of the oak and found the fat feline perched on another limb, watching her like the Cheshire cat. "I told Peter I would give Moose his antibiotic. One of the animals was having babies, I think, and he needed to be there."

"And the poor momma probably doesn't want him anywhere near her, but Peter likes to make sure everything is all right. He lost a dog and a litter of puppies because there was a complication last year. So now he personally oversees any birthing that he knows about." Noah walked toward the hose near the deck and turned the tap.

"That could be exhausting, especially during the spring."

"That's Peter. All or nothing. Actually that pretty well describes Jacob and me, too. Paul, our foster father, taught us well." He cleaned himself as best as he could under the circumstances, then offered Cara the water.

"Thanks, but I'm thinking a shower is more in line."

"If only."

"The least I can do is bring you a towel."

"Tit for tat?"

She smiled and mounted the steps of the deck. "It's dangerous to be around me. I'll get one and be right back."

Noah watched Cara disappear inside. Where in the world had that comment about being an all-or-nothing kind of guy come from? Along with knocking the breath from him, she must have rattled his brain when she landed on him. He tried to think what it was about her that—

"Here you go."

She appeared in front of him while he obviously had been in a stupor since he hadn't heard her approach. "Oh, yes, thanks."

"See you tomorrow," she said as she went back into the house.

He began drying his hair and immediately the image of her doing that a few days before popped into his head. She'd definitely rattled him. She wasn't at all like the women he dated casually. There was nothing memorable in her features—certainly nothing that normally attracted him. Especially because he never was interested in single mothers. Children and he did not mix.

One week on the job and Cara's feet still ached from standing so much. And tonight would be extra long because she would help close the restaurant for the first time. In the bathroom she slapped some water on her face, then washed her hands before heading back into the dining area to finish the last hour of her shift.

At least the tips were good. Pulling her pad out of her apron pocket to take an order, she again approached the table of three college-aged men. She pasted a smile on her face although it was an effort to keep it in place after her last encounter with them.

"You all ready to order?" She positioned herself a little farther away than usual to avoid the roaming hands of one of the customers.

"What did you say?" The massively built young man with rippling biceps who had been extra friendly slurred his words, making them run together. He bent toward her and nearly fell out of his chair.

Blasted with the scent of alcohol, she stepped back. "Are you ready to order?"

"You don't have to shout." He straightened, tossing back his head so hard his blond curls bounced.

Lord, patience is usually one of my strong suits, but this Friday night must have brought out the worst customers, and they all sat in my area of the restaurant.

Cara moved closer to the table, sidling toward the tall, thin young man sitting opposite the blond giant. "Do you all need more time to look over the menu?"

The young man brushed back a curl that fell onto his forehead. "What do you think, Brent? Jeremy? This li'l *lady* isn't being too friendly. Do we order or leave?"

"I ain't all that hungry. Let's go find a bar that's open," the one called Jeremy said, his words garbled as though he had a mouth full of pebbles.

"Bring us our bill." The blond waved his hand in the air. "We're leaving. We need to do some celebrating and you're putting a damper on our festivities." His voice rose with each sentence spoken.

Since all she had done was bring them water, she said, "There is no bill." She started to walk away, not sorry they were going, even if that meant the restaurant lost some business.

Fingers clamped about her wrist, halting her progress. She glared at the blond. "Take your hand off me."

Chapter Two

"Or what?" The blond college student shoved to his feet, swaying into her as his chair toppled over.

The sound echoed through the dining area, and several customers nearby stopped talking and stared. All three young men were standing now. The blond's huge presence dwarfed her. The odor of the alcohol they must have drunk earlier assailed her from all angles, roiling her stomach. Her heart increased its pounding against her rib cage.

The blond thrust his face close to hers, the smell intensifying. "I said, 'Or what,' li'l lady?" He mangled the words.

Speechless with fear, she tried to yank her arm away. The numbness she felt in her fingertips began to extend throughout her.

"Let go of her." The owner's deep baritone voice cut through the sudden silence.

The fingers at her wrist dug into her skin. "Whatcha gonna do about it?" The blond slowly turned his head toward Noah Maxwell, but not before Cara saw his bloodshot eyes narrow in fury.

Trying to ignore the pain his hold produced, she looked at Noah, only a few feet away. An ice-cold expression greeted her, directed at the young man gripping her. The dead calm in his eyes helped quiet her rapid heartbeat. He knew how to take care of himself. That thought eased her rising panic.

"As I thought, nothing." The blond started to turn back toward her.

"Jake—" One of his friends inched closer.

Noah settled a hand on the drunk's shoulder. "Let me show you the door, Jake."

The steel thread woven through that one sentence chilled Cara and would have made most men pause—if they hadn't been drinking and had an ounce of sense left. Jake wrenched away from Noah, still grasping her wrist, which pulled her toward the blond giant.

Cara jerked her arm toward her, hoping to throw the young man off his precarious balance. For a second he teetered, then righted himself and released his hold on her as he concentrated on Noah, who had inched even closer. His two friends came to Jake's side.

Freed, Cara hurried toward Noah, thankful it was so late that any families who usually frequented the restaurant were gone. Most of the customers had backed away, and a couple of men stayed near. She prayed they would help Noah. Jake was huge and his two friends weren't much smaller. Noah's odds didn't look good at the moment.

"We'll leave when we want. And I don't think there's too much you can do about it, old man." He glanced at his buddies, a smirk tilting his mouth. "You're outnumbered."

Noah chuckled. "Don't be too sure about that." Again that lethal quiet sounded in his voice.

Jake threw back his head and laughed. The action shifted his large body enough that he fell against one of his friends.

"I think you need to take him home," Noah said to the young man helping Jake stand upright. "Believe me when I tell you, I have been in worse situations than this and have come out unscathed."

The one called Brent took one of Jake's arms. "Let's go. Someone's probably called the police by now."

As the two dragged Jake toward the entrance, Noah quickly moved toward the trio. "I'm calling a cab to take you all home."

Brent faced him. "I'm not drunk. I can drive."

Noah assessed him. "Fine. If you don't want to end up in jail, I suggest you all go home."

Brent turned back to his friends and hooked his arm around Jake. When the door closed behind the trio, Cara sagged against a table. She couldn't stop the trembling spreading through her body.

Noah's arm went around her shoulder, supporting her against him. "Let's go back to my office."

Suddenly voices began chattering around her. She glimpsed the customers and staff staring at her and nodded. Almost in a daze, she allowed him to lead her back to his office and seat her across from him.

Thank You, Lord, for sending Noah. She folded her hands in her lap to keep them from shaking and lifted her head to look him in the eye. "Are you going to fire me?"

He looked puzzled. "Fire you? Why would I do that?"

Over the past week she'd heard wonderful things from the staff about Noah Maxwell, but she hadn't seen him enough to know him firsthand. "They'll probably never come back here to eat," she finally said when she realized he was waiting for an answer.

"Good. I don't need customers like that. I don't want drunks eating here. This is a family restaurant and I don't serve alcohol. If someone comes in again that is intoxicated, get me or the manager. You shouldn't deal with problems like that." He smiled. "I'm sorry I didn't say anything to you before, but I hadn't had to take care of something like that in a while. Most people know I don't tolerate drunks."

"Believe me, I'll have no problem doing that the next time. I appreciate your help earlier."

"My staff should never have to put up with someone like that young man." Noah relaxed in his chair. "How was your first week on the job?"

"Fine." Cara rubbed her thumb into her palm. From all accounts Noah Maxwell was a very wealthy man who still kept a personal interest in his business even though he didn't need to. He hired competent managers and most of his staff had been with him a long time.

"Are you attending the barbecue at Stone's Refuge on Sunday?" Noah asked.

"Yes, I'm helping Laura and Hannah set it up."

"Why don't you go on home?" He checked his watch. "We'll be closing up in a few minutes."

"I'm supposed to learn how to close up with Kalvin tonight."

He waved his hand. "Don't worry. You can another night. I'll help Kalvin this evening."

"But—"

"Listen, Cara—" he leaned forward, his elbows on his knees "—I know how upsetting a scene like that can be. Go home." He sat back. "Besides, I'm the boss. What I say goes."

"How can I argue with that?"

"You can't."

The smile on his face totally altered the tough-guy facade he'd presented earlier to the three men. His hazel eyes sparkled, and his dimples drew attention to the curve of his mouth. He rose slowly, pulling her gaze down his length. Dressed in a gray, long-sleeved shirt and black slacks, he commanded the space around him, as though there wasn't any situation he couldn't handle.

"Are you working tomorrow?" he asked as he opened the door for her.

"Yes, I come in at ten."

"Then you'd better go. Get some rest and put this evening behind you."

After gathering her purse, she gave him a smile over her shoulder and walked toward the exit. "Thanks. I'm still adjusting to the job. My feet are killing me."

"Try soaking them in warm saltwater."

She placed her hand on the knob and looked back at Noah. Adam, one of the high school workers, said something, and Noah turned toward him.

Weariness blanketed her. Even though the idea of warm saltwater appealed to her, she was too tired even to take the time to do that. All she wanted to do was fall into bed and sleep for hours.

She opened the back door, noticing a few other staff members gathering their belongings to leave. As she stepped outside, she relished the night air cooling her cheeks. A pool of brightness shone down from the security light. She saw Maddy, another waitress, climb into her vehicle and back out. She waved to Cara as she drove past. Cara walked toward her car, thoughts of the comfortable bed waiting for her at Laura's running through her mind.

* * *

"Boss, a toilet in the men's bathroom overflowed," one of Noah's employees said, coming from the restroom. "Will you clean it up before you leave?"

"Sure," Kalvin muttered, quickly trying to cover his frown.

Pounding at the back door drew Noah's attention. He peered through the peephole and saw Adam and Cara. Quickly he opened the door.

The ashen look on Cara's face sent alarm bells ringing in Noah's mind. "I thought both of you left. What's wrong?"

Adam gestured toward the parking lot. "Those three guys that caused problems earlier in the restaurant were waiting for Cara. They tried to drag her to their car."

Hands shaking, Cara crossed her arms over her chest. "They ran when Adam shouted at them. Or rather they staggered away. They had a liquor bottle and were passing it around. I—I didn't know—"

"I'm calling the police. Adam, did you see what they were driving? We need to report this before they kill someone."

"I want to file charges against them." Cara lifted her chin a notch. "If they had gotten me into the car…" She shuddered, closing her eyes for a few seconds.

"I'll take care of everything, Cara."

As the teen gave Noah the description of the white car, Adam shot a concerned look at Cara. "Are you all right?"

"Yes, thanks to you."

Noah was glad Adam had been at the right place at the right time, but he felt as though he had let down one of his workers. No one hurts his employees, not if he could do anything about it. He would push for those three to face the stiffest charges.

"You two can sit in my office while we wait." Noah walked to the wall phone and punched in the police department. After making his report, he said to Kalvin, "Let the officer in when he comes."

"Can we do anything to help?"

"Yeah, please finish closing up for me. I need to drive Cara home after she reports the incident."

"Okay, boss." Kalvin began to turn away, stopped and peered back at Noah. "I know Jake, Jeremy and Brent from school. They go to the University of Cimarron. They're the star players on the baseball team. Without them I doubt we'll win the conference." Kalvin headed to the kitchen.

Great! Another added bonus. Noah thought of the publicity this would trigger when the press discovered the charges the three star players would face. He didn't see any way this could be kept quiet.

He walked through the kitchen and found Cara and Adam seated in his office. While Adam peered at his hands in his lap, she stared off into space. An urge to eliminate that lost look in her eyes overwhelmed Noah. He settled in the last chair in front of his desk and faced Cara.

"The police should be here shortly. Can I get you anything until then?"

"No—yes, some water."

Adam bolted to his feet. "I'll get it."

When the teen left, Noah took Cara's trembling hands. "I'm sorry this happened. This is usually a safe place to work. I—"

"You didn't do anything. You can't control what drunks will do."

Her words plunged him back into the past. A picture

of his father striding toward him with his fist raised struck him. Those were memories he made a point of never reliving. Shoving them away, he said, "That doesn't mean I can't try."

Adam reentered the room with a law officer trailing. The teen gave Cara a glass of water and sat again in the chair next to her.

Noah stood. "Have y'all found them?"

"Right before I came in here, I got a report the three young men were pulled over not far from here. They're being taken down to headquarters to be charged with public intoxication. They'll be spending the night in jail."

Noah sighed. "Good."

"I want to file charges against them." Cara clasped the arms of her chair.

The officer removed a pad and pen. "What happened, ma'am?"

After Cara told him what had happened in the parking lot, Noah recounted the incident in the restaurant.

The police officer peered up from writing. "I'll need you all to come down and file these charges."

The exhaustion carved into Cara's face prompted Noah to ask, "Can I bring her tomorrow morning? This has been a long day for her."

"Sure, Mr. Maxwell. They won't be going anywhere." The policeman looked at Adam. "I'll need your statement, too."

"I'll bring him also," Noah said.

"You did a good thing this evening, young man." The officer said as he left.

"Since you missed your bus," Noah asked Adam, "do you need a ride home?"

Adam shook his head. "I'll get Kalvin to drive me."

"Okay. How about tomorrow to the police station?"

"No, I can take the bus. What time should I be there?"

"Nine."

Adam rose. "I'll go help Kalvin close up."

"Thanks again," Cara said as the teen hurried from the office.

"Are you ready to leave?" Noah asked.

She pushed herself to her feet, tension in every line of her body. "I have my car here."

"Since we need to go to the police station in the morning to give a statement, I'll pick you up and then bring you here so you can get your car. I'll find someone to take your shift tomorrow."

"I can come in to work tomorrow. I need the money." Anger slashed across her face. "I'm not gonna let those guys do any more to me than they already have."

Noah sensed the fear beneath the declaration. Any moment he expected her to fall apart. "I don't think you should drive yourself home. Your hands are shaking."

The urge to draw her against him and hold her until her fear subsided set off alarms in Noah's mind. He would take her home and to the police tomorrow because he was her employer. Even a temporary employee deserved his support. But after that, he would go his way and she hers. He made it a practice never to get involved with a single mother, and he intended to keep his life uncomplicated.

"Let's go. It's been a long day." Noah withdrew his car keys from his pocket. When she started to protest, he cut her off. "Humor me. I wouldn't be able to sleep if I sent you to Laura's by yourself."

Cara took a deep breath, then released it slowly. "Fine, but I'm coming into work tomorrow." Her shoulders sagged as though suddenly she couldn't keep the exhaustion at bay.

"If that's the way you want it." Maybe nothing would come of charging the star baseball players. Although he hadn't known what the three guys looked like, he'd heard their names. For the first time in years, the team had a chance to win big because of these players. Who was he kidding? It was going to be a mess. This town was sports crazy when it came to supporting the University of Cimarron City Tigers. And Cara would be in the middle of it. He needed to warn her.

They settled in his Corvette, and for ten minutes, Noah negotiated the streets in silence. He didn't know how to tell her who the young men were and just how popular they were in town.

Hesitant to make matters worse, he settled on something he remembered Laura saying about Cara. "Why does Laura call you a free spirit?"

Her laughter was forced. "She was being sarcastic. I'm anything but that."

"But you left St. Louis on the spur of the moment?"

"Yeah, that was out of character. I normally plan everything down to the tiniest detail."

"We all do things out of character from time to time." *Like what I'm doing now. I don't get involved with women like Cara, women who want commitment. Ever.*

"I guess it really wasn't on the spur of the moment. Laura had been working on getting me here for the last eighteen months. So when Timothy said he missed Matthew and Joshua and playing with them, I decided it was time to move." She leaned her head back on the soft leather cushion and closed her eyes. "I don't want to return to St. Louis."

Her comment out of the blue took him by surprise. "Why not?" he asked, before his internal censor could stop him from delving into her personal life.

"There's nothing there for me. It was never my home."

"How long did you live there?"

"Four years. Almost two after my husband died."

"Where did you live before that?" He increased his speed once they left the city. Only five more minutes to the farm. Obviously his censor was defective this evening.

"I grew up in Flagstaff." She straightened as he turned onto the road that led to Peter and Laura's. "I was actually thinking of going there when I got in the car, but came here instead."

"Why did you change your mind?" One minute away. He never got this personal with a woman, even the superficial ones he usually dated who never threatened his marital status. Too risky.

"I didn't want to admit I couldn't make it on my own. When Tim died, my parents wanted me to come home so they could take care of me. I haven't even told them yet I'm in Cimarron City."

He pulled to a stop in front of Peter's house. A sigh escaped his lips. "I'll pick you up a little before nine. It shouldn't take too long at the police station."

"I hope not. I don't want to spend any more time than I have to on those three."

The urge to drive away quickly assailed him. But he couldn't leave yet. He had to tell her who those three were. When she opened the door and the light came on, Noah twisted to face her. Fatigue dulled the green in her eyes while her forehead wrinkled in question.

"You should know who Jake, Jeremy and Brent are before we go down to the station tomorrow."

Her mouth pinched into a frown. "I know they're boys parading around as men. They need to be held accountable for their actions."

"I agree. But they're the three star baseball players at the university here. Many of the townspeople have lived vicariously through their accomplishments."

She smoothed a wisp of blond hair back from her plain-looking face. "Are you saying they should get special treatment?" Fury invaded her voice.

"No, I'm saying that the press may be all over this, and I want you to be prepared."

She slid from the front seat and leaned down to look at him. "Consider me prepared. Thanks for the ride and the help tonight."

The stiff way she carried herself toward the house spoke of her aggravation, some of it probably directed at him. He was afraid the justice she wanted wouldn't happen, that she was going to be hurt further.

He waited while she slipped inside the house, wishing he could take care of the situation without involving her. His hands tightened on the steering wheel as he pictured Cara, vulnerable, trying to act brave. Most of his adult life he had avoided commitment. What was it about Cara Winters that made him think twice about his decision years ago to go it alone in this world?

Saturday afternoon after reconciling his receipts from the night before, Noah came to the conclusion one of his employees was stealing from him—to the tune of forty dollars for the second time this week. That knowledge made his stomach clench. He had thought it was an honest mistake. After all, he treated his employees fairly. Now it was obvious that was wishful thinking on his part.

In his youth he'd been tempted to steal in order to have money to eat. Instead, he'd gotten a job and, when that wasn't enough, he'd gone out for a second one. When he got his hands on the thief, he would bring charges against that person.

He made his way to the dining room, trying to decide what to do to catch the thief. His gaze lit upon Cara near the waitress station. The circles under her eyes stood out against her pale cheeks. For a split second he had an urge to smooth them away. Instead he walked over and took two of her drinks. "Isn't it time for your break?"

"As soon as I take care of table twenty."

He held up the water. "I'll help you. Are these for them?"

Her mouth formed a hard line. "I can do it."

"I know you can." He grinned. "Indulge me. I'd feel better if I helped."

"Why?"

"Because it's been a long day, especially with having to go to the police station this morning. You shouldn't be here at work and I let you come anyway."

She stepped close, her scent of vanilla wafting to him. "I'm not fragile. I won't break." She plucked the glasses from his grasp and put then on a tray. She scooted around him and walked toward the front of the restaurant.

I guess she put me in my place. He watched her interact with the family at table twenty. A little girl about six said something to Cara. When Cara smiled, her whole face radiated joy. Her green eyes even twinkled. The child laughed and all traces of fatigue momentarily disappeared from Cara's expression. Her plain features transformed in a beautiful countenance.

What am I doing? I have no business standing here

eyeing Cara when I have a thief to catch. Noah scanned the pizzeria, studying each employee who had worked the night before. Kalvin was cleaning off a table in the corner. Adam was ringing up an order. And Cara had finished with table twenty and was heading toward the kitchen. One of them was a thief.

He couldn't see it being Cara. She was a friend of Laura's. Besides, she hadn't worked the first time money was missing. If it wasn't her, it had to be Kalvin or Adam. They were hard workers and had been with him for almost a year. He hated thinking the thief was either one of them. He pivoted toward the kitchen. All he could do was keep an eye on both teens. He would be there waiting when the thief made a mistake.

Noah planted himself in the corner by the soft drink dispenser. He had a clear view of the cash register, but couldn't be seen.

Not twenty minutes passed when a commotion in the main dining room drew him out.

"Watch where you're going, lady."

Lisa, one of his waitresses, hovered over a dropped tray, shards of broken dishes strewn across the floor. "I'm sorry."

Grumbling under his breath, the man walked toward the entrance.

Cara paused with two iced teas next to Noah. "He ran into Lisa. It wasn't her fault."

He smiled at the woman who had haunted his thoughts way too much lately. "Thanks."

Cara placed the drinks in front of a couple, then made her way to Lisa and bent down to help the young woman clean up the mess.

Satisfied everything was all right, Noah turned away.

Out of the corner of his eye, he caught a glimpse of Adam quickly stuffing some money into his pocket while he stood in front of the cash register. The teen looked up and their gazes collided. Adam's nostrils flared, his expression guilt-ridden.

He slammed the drawer close and spun around, hurrying toward the back. Noah followed. Halfway across the kitchen, the teen broke into a run and shoved out the door.

Noah gave chase. Outside he checked the area and saw the teen sprinting across the side parking lot, toward the street. Noah rushed after him, thankful he kept in good shape with jogging.

"Adam! Stop!"

Throwing a glance over his shoulder, Adam changed course and darted to the left. Noah mirrored the teen's action.

Suddenly the boy altered his direction again, swinging to the right. He dashed across the street toward the park. Noah thought of all the hiding places in the wooded area and pushed himself even faster.

In the park, Adam headed toward a grove of trees along an access road. He chanced a look back at Noah. Quickly turning forward again, the teen veered right into the path of an oncoming car speeding around a curve.

The screech of the tires on the pavement reverberated through Noah as he witnessed Adam being clipped by the car and thrown forward into the dirt along the side of the road. For a second, shock slowed his pace. Adam lay sprawled half in the grass and half in the graveled shoulder. Not moving. Staring up at the sky.

All thoughts of what happened at his restaurant fled Noah's mind as he raced toward the youth, his heart pounding as fast as his feet on the ground. The car slowed for a few seconds while the vehicle's occupants were probably checking out what had happened. Noah couldn't tell for certain because dark tinted glass hid the car's interior.

As Noah neared Adam, the tan sedan gunned forward. Noah noted the first three letters of the license plate before the vehicle disappeared, nearly hitting a truck parked at the curb.

Noah scanned the area for help. Empty paths and a deserted road greeted his inspection. Not sure what to do, he knelt next to Adam. The boy gasped for air, his eyes wide with fear. He peered at Noah, blinked, then tried to move. A cry pierced the quiet.

Noah laid his hands on Adam's shoulders. "Stay still. I'm getting you help."

"No! I can't..." The boy shifted, his eyes fluttering closed before popping open again.

Noah dug into his pocket for his cell. He called 9-1-1 and quickly told the dispatcher where to find them. "Adam?"

The teen sucked in a shallow breath, a moan escaping from his lips.

"Where do you hurt?"

"My leg." He clenched his teeth and struggled to prop himself up on his elbows to take a look.

"Stay still. An ambulance is on its way."

"I need to get home." Adam collapsed back to the ground, his features pale, his teeth chattering. "I can't go to the hospital."

"Don't worry. I'll take care of everything." In the distance Noah heard a siren.

Reassured help was on the way, he glanced around again to see if anyone else was nearby. He spied Cara jogging toward them about thirty yards away. Relief went through him.

When Noah looked back at Adam, the teen had rolled over and shoved himself to his feet. The boy tried to hobble away, but fell after taking only two steps and screamed when both knees hit the dirt. Noah scrambled forward to ease him down onto the ground.

"I told you not to worry about anything." Although he was concerned about the teen's injuries, Noah schooled his voice into a soothing cadence.

Adam lifted a tear-streaked face to Noah. "I can't go to the hospital. I have to get home. I have—"

"I'll call your dad and let him know what happened. He'll need to meet us at the hospital."

The teen's eyes grew even rounder, panic replacing the apprehension in them. "No!"

"I won't tell your dad about you stealing money from me. Let's just forget that. What's your number?" Noah could feel Cara's comforting presence behind him; he could hear her panting as she caught her breath.

Pain twisted Adam's face. "He's not home."

"Where does he work? I'll call him there then." Noah raised his voice to be heard over the siren blaring from the ambulance that came to a stop nearby.

Adam clamped his lips together, tears continuing to run down his cheeks.

"Adam?" Now kneeling beside them, Cara placed her hand on the boy's arm. "We need to let your family know what's happened."

The gentle tone of her voice erased some of the tension in the teen's expression. Adam looked toward her. He started to say something, but instead snapped his mouth closed and averted his head.

Two paramedics approached with the stretcher, stooped and began examining Adam. Noah and Cara rose and stepped back to give them room.

A police officer approached. "Can you tell me what happened here?"

Noah relayed the events to the man while keeping his gaze on Adam. This was his fault. He shouldn't have chased the teen. He should have let it go.

"I'll report your description of the car and see if we can find it." The officer walked back to his vehicle to call it in.

The paramedics lifted Adam onto the stretcher and secured him. They started wheeling him toward the ambulance.

"Wait! Mr. Maxwell," Adam called out.

Noah hurried toward the stretcher. "Yes? What's your dad's number?"

"He's gone. My brother and sister will be by themselves. They'll get scared. Please..." He shifted as though he needed to sit up. He winced and groaned.

"I'll take care of them. Don't worry about them. Where's your dad?"

The teen closed his eyes. The paramedics hefted the stretcher into the back of the ambulance.

Noah heard the teen say, "Out of town." Then the door shut.

With dusk descending, Cara stared down at the address written on the paper then back up at the number on the mailbox that leaned against the curb, propped up by several large rocks. "This is it."

Sitting in the passenger seat, Noah stared at the house that easily could be described as a shack. What paint remained on the wooden structure had turned a dull gray, and two of the windows were missing a pane while one of the steps up to the sagging porch was broken.

Sweat coated his forehead and beaded his upper lip. Transported back twenty years ago, Noah remembered, that last time he'd come home as though it had transpired yesterday. He would never be rid of the memory. It would haunt him to his dying day.

"This place doesn't even look safe." Cara pushed her door open.

"We'll get his brother and sister and take them to the hospital. We can leave a note for his dad. Adam said he was out of town. Hopefully just for the day."

"Have you met either of them?"

"His younger brother. He's come by the restaurant several times while I've been there. I let Rusty help out in the back until Adam was ready to leave."

"Good. Then he'll know you." Cara mounted the stairs, stepping over the one that lay in two pieces.

Noah knocked. Sounds of a television competed with a dog's barking. A minute crawled by. Then another. He started to pound on the wood again when the door swung open. A little girl, with big blue eyes and long blond hair, stared up at Noah. She held a stuffed bear with a missing button eye and part of his brown fur rubbed off in several places.

Not knowing the girl's name, Noah said, "Hi. Is your brother home?"

She slammed the door in his face.

Chapter Three

Cara stepped in front of Noah. "Let me try. You can be pretty intimidating." She raised her hand to knock when the door opened again. This time a taller boy, maybe nine years old, with red hair and freckles stood in the entrance. "Rusty?"

The child frowned at Cara. "We don't want—"

Noah stepped into view. "Rusty, do you remember me? I'm Adam's boss at the restaurant."

The boy swept his gaze to Noah and nodded.

"Adam has been taken to the hospital. He was hurt. We told him we'd take you and your sister to see him," Noah explained.

"He's hurt? How?" Rusty asked, wide-eyed.

"He was hit by a car," Noah said.

The boy blinked, all color draining from his face.

Cara came between the two. "I'm Cara, Rusty. I work with Adam. He'll be all right once he's patched up at the hospital. Why don't you get your sister, and you two will be able to see for yourselves."

"We'll just write your dad a note in case he comes back," Noah said over Cara's shoulder.

Rusty's mouth twisted. "He ain't coming back."

"What do you mean?" Cara asked, drawing the boy's attention back to her.

Noah moved into the house and surveyed the place. The inside was as bad as the outside. Off to the side in the living room, the little girl lounged on a brown couch with its stuffing spilling out of various tears. The only other furniture was two wooden cartons stacked together as a table, on which the television sat.

Noah looked back at the boy in time to see him shrug.

"Ain't supposed to say," Rusty said.

Cara came into the house. "We'll write him a note anyway. Can you get me some paper?" She rummaged in her purse and withdrew a pen.

Rusty stared at Cara for a long moment, as though trying to decide what to do. Finally he dug into a backpack by the front door. He ripped a sheet from a notebook then gave it to her.

While Cara scribbled a message to the children's father, Noah walked into the kitchen and inspected the refrigerator. A quart of chocolate milk and a pizza carton from his restaurant were the only items on the bottom shelf. The top one held a few slices of American cheese and several pint-size boxes of apple juice.

When he shut the door and turned, he found Rusty staring at him with wariness in his eyes. "Not much in the fridge."

"Nope." The boy dropped his gaze.

Something was definitely wrong here. Noah opened a cupboard and discovered bare shelves. Some dishes were stacked in the next one. In the third cabinet one cereal box, a jar of peanut butter and a loaf of bread sent off alarms in his mind. Were the children living here by themselves? Was that why Adam had been in such a panic to get home? Why Rusty wasn't supposed to talk about where his father was?

Cara entered the kitchen; the concern in her gaze reflected his own. "I left the note on top of the TV."

Noah nodded. "Are you all ready to go, Rusty?"

"Are you sure Adam is gonna be okay?" the boy asked, his teeth biting into his lower lip.

"Yes, the doctor will take good care of Adam." Noah strode to the child and clasped his shoulder. "Let's go."

Rusty didn't move, a serious expression on his face. "We ain't got any money for a doctor."

Noah smiled reassuringly. "Don't you worry about that. I'm taking care of the doctor. I told the paramedics that." He felt a tug and peered behind him.

Adam's little sister tilted her head, her eyes huge, and asked, "Can I bring Molly?"

"Molly?"

"Our puppy," the little girl said.

Noah looked around. "Where's Molly?"

"Rusty put her in the back room when you knocked. We don't want no one to take her from us."

"Can you show me where Molly is?" Cara asked, holding out her hand for the little girl to take.

She fitted her small fingers in Cara's grasp and pulled Cara toward a door to the left. "Molly's in there." A scratching sound came from the other side of the wood. "She'll want out. She doesn't like staying in there." The girl paused, her hand on the knob.

"What's your name?" Cara stood behind the child.

"Lindsay."

"That's such a pretty name."

"My mama gave it to me."

"Where's your mama?" Cara asked.

"In heaven. That's what Papa told me." Lindsay slowly turned the knob. "I have to be real careful when I open the door. Molly likes to bolt."

"You'd better keep it closed, Lindsay. She likes to jump up on strangers." Rusty covered the distance between them and drew away his sister's hand. "Molly will be okay till we get back. Let's go bring Adam home."

Lindsay's stomach growled. "Yeah, I'm gettin' hungry."

Noah followed the trio out to Cara's car. After the kids were settled in the back, he slid into the front passenger seat. "Buckle up."

Cara pulled away from the curb. "Let's go to a fast-food-drive-through and pick up something for you two to eat." She glanced back at the children. "Okay?"

"Can I have a hamburger and fries?" Rusty asked.

"I'm crushed. Not a pizza?" Noah said.

Lindsay leaned toward Noah. "I'll tell ya a secret. I'm kinda sick of pizza. We have that almost every night. Adam brings it home when he works."

"Then burgers and fries it is." Noah caught Cara's look. "Thanks for driving. My sports car isn't kid friendly."

She chuckled. "Oh, I don't know about that. I imagine there are some big kids who would love to drive a Corvette around."

"As your boss I'm gonna ignore that barb. I'm not going through a second childhood. I've always had a Corvette since I could afford it."

"Ah, so you never outgrew your first one."

"Ouch," Noah said, studying the way her smile changed her face. Her green eyes glittered as though sun rays kissed the new spring grass. But it wasn't her eyes that he was attracted to when she smiled. Her full lips, curving upward, lured him away from them and kept him transfixed.

After picking up food for the children, Noah listened to sounds from the back. The rustling of the paper bags. The slurping of their drinks. The quiet while they ate.

When the two finished, Rusty and Lindsay began whispering between themselves. Noah glimpsed the fear in their expressions. He imagined he'd had that same look on his face many times while he'd been growing up. Rusty tried to mask his worry with a brave, tough front, but it was there in the way he bit into his lower lip or nibbled on his thumb.

At the hospital Rusty held his little sister's hand as they all walked toward the emergency entrance. Noah hung back and gestured toward Cara to do likewise.

"I don't think there's a father around anymore. I met him once, but that was a while back."

"That could explain why all of a sudden Adam is stealing money. There wasn't much at the house."

"Yeah, that makes sense. I know their father worked at a place where there was health insurance." Noah slanted a look toward the two children at the glass doors, waiting for them. "But if he's left them, that insurance may no longer be in effect. They'll need help. Thankfully I have some connections."

"The authorities will have to be notified."

"I know." He made a gesture with his head toward the kids. "They won't like it."

Cara strode toward the children with a smile on her face. "Let's go see Adam."

Chewing on his thumbnail, Rusty hesitated. "Adam will be okay?"

Noah advanced toward the trio. "Of course. Nothing can get your brother down for long."

Lindsay went inside, standing on the other side of the sliding glass doors. "C'mon, Rusty. I wanna see Adam." She clutched her teddy bear to her, her eyes round, all her anxiety apparent.

Noah gritted his teeth. He'd caused that fear. Somehow he had to right this wrong.

"Don't cry, Lindy," Adam murmured in a weak voice, his eyelids drooping.

"I don't wanna leave ya." Lindsay's sobs permeated the hospital room.

The sound tightened Cara's chest, as if she couldn't get a decent breath. Children's Protective Services would be here shortly to pick up both Lindsay and Rusty to go to the shelter. Noah was in the hall, making one call after another about their situation. But it looked as though, even with his connections, the two kids would be leaving soon while Adam lay in the hospital bed, drowsy from the surgery to repair his broken leg.

Lindsay clung to Adam while Rusty stood behind her protectively, scowling as though he was too angry to talk. The second he'd realized where he and his sister would be staying the night he'd clammed up. Her heart went out to him. Rusty was only a year older than her own son, Timothy. Every time she looked at the boy, she wondered how her son would deal with this kind of situation. He'd always been shielded, even when her life had started falling apart.

The door swished open, and she turned, expecting to see someone from Children's Protective Services. Instead, thankfully, Noah entered the room, but his expression didn't bode well for Rusty and Lindsay.

Noah came to Cara's side, observing the three siblings talking in lowered voices. When he turned his back on them, he cleared his throat and said, "I got them to let me take them to Stone's Refuge for the night at Hannah and Jacob's house."

"Good."

"But it's only temporary. All three cottages are full. As it is, they'll be sleeping on cots."

"So the refuge isn't an option for them?" Cara glanced at the children, Lindsay's face buried in the crook of Adam's arm while Rusty glared at Noah and her.

"Not at this time. Even if it became available, I can't see three places opening at the same time. And they wouldn't be able to stay in the same cottage."

"What are the chances of them being sent to the same foster home?" Cara lowered her voice even more, feeling the heat of Rusty's anger from across the room.

"The supervisor I know at Children's Protective Services didn't give me much hope of keeping them together."

She closed her eyes for a few seconds, the weariness she'd fought for the past few hours starting to catch up with her.

"Can you drive me back to the restaurant to pick up my car and then take them to the farm? I'll follow you."

"Yes, of course." Another quick glance toward the three siblings cemented her determination to do what she could for them. They had been through so much. And she owed Adam for what he had done the night before. "How do you suggest we get them to leave?"

"I was gonna ask you that. You're the expert."

"Expert! Whatever made you think that?"

"You have a child. I don't."

"Well, for your information, nothing has quite prepared me for this kind of situation."

His grin, with his two dimples emerging, encompassed his whole face. "I know for a fact you're a quick study. You picked up waitressing in no time."

She planted her hand on her waist. "Just in case you haven't figured it out, this is entirely different. I—"

"We aren't leaving." Rusty cut into their conversation.

Cara faced the children, Lindsay holding Adam's hand and Rusty gripping hers. A united front.

The nine-year-old pointed toward the couch. "We can sleep there."

Lindsay drew herself up as tall as possible. "Yeah!"

"They need to stay with me." Adam's eyelids drifted closed. Then as if he realized he was falling asleep, he opened them wide. "Dad will…be back. I'm to take care…of them until…he returns which…" His voice faded as his head sagged to the side, his eyes shut again.

"He needs to get his rest if he's going to get better." Cara quickly covered the distance to the kids and placed her hand on Rusty's shoulder.

He jerked away. "No, we're staying!"

Lindsay backed up against the bed, gripping her stuffed animal so tightly her knuckles whitened. "I don't wanna leave! I don't wanna leave!" Tears coursed down her cheeks.

Cara knelt in front of the little girl, her own tears close

to the surface at the heart-wrenching sounds. "Adam needs rest to get better. I promise you two I'll bring you back tomorrow to see him." She smoothed the child's dirty hair back from her face. "I never break a promise. You will see Adam tomorrow."

"In the morning?" Lindsay asked between sobs. "First thing?"

"Yes." Cara looked over at Rusty watching them. "He'll need to know you two are being taken care of while he has to stay here and get well."

Pouting, Rusty gnawed on his thumbnail.

Cara straightened and presented her hand to Lindsay. "Ready to go?"

The little girl nodded, grasping Cara's forefinger.

On the drive to the farm, in the rearview mirror, Cara saw Lindsay slump against her brother and fall asleep. But the whole way to Stone's Refuge, Rusty kept his gaze trained out the side window, staring into the darkness, his jaw set in a firm line.

The closer she came to Laura and Peter's farm where Stone's Refuge was, the wearier Cara became. She tightened her hands about the steering wheel to keep her arms from dropping to her lap as though they were deadweight. Noah's headlights following behind her car comforted her as they left the brightness of the city.

She pulled onto the gravel road that led to the three cottages that housed the foster children and Hannah and Jacob's home. The lights up ahead beckoned her with the promise of hope.

Father, please find a home for Lindsay, Rusty and Adam to live together. I have a feeling they have gone through a lot in their short lives. They need stability. A place to call home. A place to put down roots. In Jesus Christ's name. Amen.

Cara parked in front of a two-story house, which was ablaze with lights even though it was well after two in the morning. The minute she climbed from her car, the door opened and both Hannah and Jacob came outside.

Noah lifted Lindsay into his arms and carried her up the steps to the porch with Rusty reluctantly trailing behind the pair. Cara took up the rear, watching as Hannah and Jacob welcomed Noah and the children.

I want a home. I want stability, too, Father. Is this the place for me or should I move on? Show me Your will.

Hannah stayed behind the others and welcomed Cara. "It's good to see you again. Laura made me promise to call her the second y'all arrived. She's been worried with everything that has happened lately."

The mention of the past thirty-six hours caused Cara to falter. She grasped the doorjamb and steadied herself.

"Go on home. I can take it from here. You look beat." Hannah practically blocked Cara's entry into the cottage. "That's not a suggestion," she added in a no-nonsense voice.

When Cara entered Laura's house at the other end of the farm a few minutes later, thankfully her friend didn't meet her at the door, wanting to know what had occurred with Adam. She wasn't up to any explanations. Tomorrow would come soon enough.

In the den Cara pulled the hide-away bed out of the couch and collapsed onto the covers without removing her clothes. Sleep immediately whisked her away, and the next thing she knew someone was shaking her awake.

"Mom, you need to get ready for church."

Cara opened her eyes to a room bright with sunlight

and stared up at her eight-year-old son, who loomed over her. Tiny frown lines creased his forehead.

"What time is it, honey?"

"Almost eight."

She held her groan inside, but she wanted to roll over and pull the covers over her head. Five hours sleep wasn't enough.

"Why are you dressed to go to work? I thought you were off today," Timothy asked, pointing to her wrinkled shirt and pants.

Cara forced a smile to her lips, cutting off the yawn building in her. "I'm off. I've got to help Laura this afternoon with the barbecue at Stone's Refuge. Before that, honey, I promised a little girl I would take her to see her brother in the hospital."

"Is that the person who got hurt at work?"

"How did you know about that?"

"I overheard Laura talking to Peter about an accident at work." Anxiety that Cara hadn't seen in the past few months darkened her son's brown eyes. "I was scared it was you, but Laura told me it was one of the teenagers working at the restaurant."

Cara hugged Timothy to her, kissing the top of his head. "Don't you know, nothing could take me away from you? You're stuck with me." For the first year after her husband died from a long, painful illness, her son would awaken every night drenched in sweat, crying out for her. Slowly the nightmares disappeared when he realized she wasn't going to leave him, but every once in a while she saw the fear in his eyes.

Timothy leaned back and grinned. "I don't mind. You're a pretty good mom."

"Just pretty good?" She tackled him to the bed and

began tickling his sides. His laughter chased away the problems of the past few days—until a knock interrupted their horseplay.

"Come in," she called out as she sat on the edge of the bed.

Laura poked her head in. "Hannah just called. Rusty and Lindsay are gone."

Chapter Four

Once out of the city limits, Noah pressed down on the accelerator. He should have realized Rusty and Lindsay would try something like running away. He'd done his share of that while in foster homes and would have while living with his father if it hadn't been for his kid sister. He couldn't leave her there alone with their dad, and there wasn't any way he would have risked taking her out on the streets.

A picture of the last time he'd seen Whitney, crying, waving goodbye, popped into his mind. He gritted his teeth.

Where are you? Why can't I find you? The last report from the private investigator he'd hired to search for Whitney hadn't been promising. The man only had a couple of more leads to follow before he would call it quits.

Wrapped up in his thoughts, Noah had to look twice to realize two kids had darted behind some bushes alongside the highway. He saw a glimpse of pink among the foliage. He hoped it was Lindsay and Rusty.

He parked a few yards from the large shrubbery and climbed from his Corvette. A squeak erupted from behind the bush, then a redheaded boy, dragging a little girl with blond hair, dashed out and ran in the opposite direction. Not again!

"Stop, Rusty and Lindsay!"

They kept going. Noah took after them, his long legs chewing up the distance between them.

When he was a few feet from them, he noticed Rusty glancing across the highway. "Don't do anything dangerous, Rusty."

At that moment a pickup came over a rise and whizzed by them. The boy slowed, his chest rising and falling rapidly. When he stopped, he bent over and pulled air into his lungs.

Lindsay did likewise, tears streaking down her face. "My side hurts." She held it and plopped down on the gravel shoulder.

Another vehicle sped past them. Noah picked up Lindsay and moved her back from the road. Rusty collapsed next to his sister, looking daggers at Noah. He ignored them and sat on the other side of Lindsay, propping himself up on his elbows.

Noah waited until their breathing returned to normal, then asked, "Where were you all going?"

Rusty stuck his lower lip out. "Home. I'm sure Dad will be home by now."

"He's not coming home. Adam told me he'd left for good."

"No! Daddy wouldn't do that!" Lindsay began crying.

Noah looked at the little girl, not sure what to do. He'd always thought the truth was the best way to go, but listening to the child's sobs tore his heart. He started to reach for Lindsay to comfort her when Rusty shoved his hand away.

"See what you did! You upset my sister!" The boy wrapped his arm around Lindsay and brought her to him.

Okay, he'd always known he wasn't good with small children. Teenagers worked for him so he could deal with them, but this was way out of the realm of his expertise. What should he do?

Call Cara. She would know. He remembered how she had managed to calm them yesterday on a number of occasions. She was a natural. He dug his cell out of his pocket and called Peter's house. When no one answered, he tried Jacob's. Hannah answered on the third ring.

"Is Cara there?" Noah slid a glance toward the two beside him. He wouldn't put it past them to try escaping again.

When Cara came on the phone, Noah sighed. "I'm sitting here with Rusty and Lindsay on the side of the highway about five minutes away from the farm. Can you pick them up? I don't have room in my car."

"Sure. I'll be there in a minute."

Noah snapped his cell closed, then suddenly wondered why he hadn't just asked Hannah to come get the kids. Why had he asked Cara? She had a history with them. That was it! Certainly not because he wanted to see her.

"We'll run away again. We ain't going back there. We're going home." Rusty's angry words cut into Noah's rationalization.

Noah knew the next and last time they would go to that house was to pick up their belongings. It should be torn down or at the very least declared a disaster zone.

Lindsay jerked her head up, wet tracks on her thin cheeks. "Molly! She's alone at the house."

The puppy. He'd forgotten about her. "The farm will be a great place for her to live. There are a lot of animals and a lot of children to love them."

Terror widened the little girl's eyes. "She's mine! I love her!"

He was batting zero. "I promise I will go get her and bring her to see you."

Lindsay's had a determined expression. "To keep."

Again Noah kept his mouth shut. Thankfully he usually learned pretty quickly.

"Adam gave her to me." The little girl's eyes drilled into him.

Noah shifted under the children's glares. Although it was in the fifties, sweat broke out on his forehead. At that moment the sound of a car pulling up sent such a bolt of relief through him he nearly collapsed to the ground.

He jumped up, dusting off his khaki pants, and swung around. Cara hurried toward them.

"Are you guys all right?" She directed the question at the children, kneeling down in front of them.

Lindsay stabbed a finger toward Noah. "*He* says we can't go home, that Daddy is gone for good. He won't let me have Molly, either." Tears glistened in the little girl's blue eyes.

He felt like a heel, and he really hadn't done anything wrong. *Is this how having children makes a person feel?* No wonder he didn't want to have anything to do with having a family.

Cara brushed the child's blond hair behind her ears. "I was coming over to take you to see Adam like I promised."

"We got tired of waiting for you." Rusty's pout returned in full force.

"It's only eight-thirty."

"We've been up for hours, dressed and ready to go." The boy gnawed on the end of his thumb.

"Did you get any sleep?" Cara peered from Lindsay to Rusty, such kindness in her eyes that Noah wished she would look at him like that.

No! Strike that! I have no business thinking that.

Rusty's mutinous expression spoke volumes—that and the weary look in his eyes. Obviously they hadn't slept at all. He could certainly have used a few more hours himself. After returning home last night, he'd been so keyed up that it had taken him several hours finally to fall asleep.

Cara rose. "Let's go see Adam. I'm sure he will be feeling a lot better this morning and will want to see you two."

Lindsay leaped to her feet and took Cara's hand. Rusty stood reluctantly. He trudged behind Cara and Lindsay as they headed for her Chevy.

After the children were secured in the car, Cara turned toward Noah and smiled. "Are you coming with us?"

He was ninety percent sure he heard Rusty mutter no, but he took it as a challenge. There wasn't anything he couldn't do if he put his mind to it. "Yes. I'll follow you to the hospital."

"See you there." Cara slipped behind the steering wheel and pulled out onto the highway.

Now why had he done that? He was committed to going to the hospital with two—no, make that three—children who weren't too happy with him right at the moment.

Later that afternoon, a stale musky smell drifted to him as Noah stepped inside Adam's house. Frantic barking accompanied him to the kitchen. Carefully he inched the door open to where Molly was kept. He thought he had prepared himself for the large puppy, but before he realized it she barged through the narrow gap and raced around the room, the barking so loud it echoed and bounced around in his brain.

What possessed him to volunteer to pick up Molly while Cara took Rusty and Lindsay back to Stone's Refuge?

Finally the puppy paused, her tongue lolling to the side as she panted. After studying him for a few seconds, she rushed toward him and jumped up on him, pinning him back against the counter. She licked him everywhere she could reach. Thankfully she wasn't full grown yet or his face would have been bathed. As it was, after he managed to disengage himself from her, his blue shirt was damp and her doggie smell stuck to his clothes—not a particularly pleasant scent.

When Molly started to launch herself at him again, he quickly held her back. "Nice, Molly. Stay." He added the last in a stern voice as if that would make a difference to the animal.

Her tail wagging, she peered up at him as though he was her new best friend, her rescuer. Keeping his hand out, he surveyed the kitchen and didn't see a leash.

"What am I supposed to do?" he asked the mixed breed with a good dose of German shepherd in her.

She barked once. He glanced toward the room where she stayed. With an eye on her, he sidled toward the door and flipped on the light. Other than two bowls, one with a few pieces of kibble and the other with an inch of water, the small space was vacant.

He must have taken his attention off her because the

next thing he realized the puppy nudged his hand, her cold nose buried in his palm. He'd never had a pet while he was growing up and he didn't have one now. He wasn't home enough to be a good pet owner, and if he did something, he always did it well. He definitely felt out of his element, but all he had to do was get Molly to the farm and Jacob and Peter could take over. They were naturals with animals.

After sizing Molly up, he came to the conclusion there was only one way to get her to his car. He stooped over and slid his arms under her belly. Surprised at how much she weighed—at least fifty pounds, he guessed—he lifted the puppy, cradling her against his chest, and started for his Corvette.

At the front door he struggled to open it with Molly in his embrace. He received a wet tongue in the face for his efforts. All he had to do was get her to his vehicle, and he would be home free. Again he mulled over how to get her inside the Corvette without letting her go. Pressing her against the car's side, he held her in place with his body as he fumbled for the handle.

He practically stumbled into the vehicle with the puppy tumbling out of his arms. He quickly slammed the door before she escaped. Between licking all around the open window she yelped, the sound chasing him all the way back to the house where he quickly locked up, then returned to the Corvette.

Twenty minutes and he would be free to enjoy the rest of the afternoon at Stone Refuge's barbecue. The occasional wet nose against his face spurred him to go a little faster than usual. He pulled into the farm sixteen minutes later and nearly drove off the road when Molly barked in his ear.

"Are you determined I join Adam in the hospital?" he asked the animal.

Another loud yap greeted his question, ringing in his head. He parked next to Peter's truck. As Noah climbed from his Corvette, a mob of children surrounded him, preventing him from moving.

The puppy bolted from the car, barreling through the mass of kids. "Molly!" He imagined having to tell Lindsay he'd lost her pet, so he dived toward the animal and landed facedown in the dirt.

Laughter penetrated his dazed mind as he rolled over and looked up at all the giggling children. Cara's face suddenly filled his vision, concern knitting her forehead. Not his finest moment.

"Are you all right?" she asked over the children's sounds of glee.

The kids dispersed, leaving him relatively alone with Cara, who offered him assistance up. "Where's Molly?" He scanned the area. "Did she run off?"

Merriment danced in her eyes. "No, Peter caught her and put a leash on her, then took her to the barn where Rusty and Lindsay are."

He clasped her hand and let her tug him to his feet. "After the past few days' exertion, my body is beginning to protest." Rolling his head and shoulders, he released her grasp and immediately missed her touch—soft and warm, the complete opposite of the ground he'd encountered a moment before. "Where is everyone?"

She pointed toward the barn. "When you pulled up, the kids were heading there to help feed the animals. Hannah and Laura are in the house with your foster mother, finishing up the food preparation."

"So Jacob and Peter are with the children?"

"Yes."

"Then I guess I'd better join them."

"You can always help cook."

He splayed his hand over his heart. "Just because I own a chain of restaurants doesn't mean I know how to cook beyond pizza and sandwiches."

Both eyebrows rose. "You don't?"

He shook his head. "I can make a few things, but I rarely eat at home. I'm usually at one of my restaurants. About the only time I get a home-cooked meal is when I visit Jacob or Peter. I'm thankful their wives are good cooks."

"That's a shame."

"No, that's just how things are." He glanced toward the barn. "I'd better go check and see if they need any help."

As he limped away, Cara called out, "Thanks for picking up Molly."

He turned and backpedaled, warmed by the grin she gave him. "Any time I can be of service."

As he walked along the gravel road to the barn, he felt her gaze on him and wondered what she was thinking. He smiled when he remembered her in her apron, helping him up, a smudge of chocolate on her cheek. He'd been tempted to ki—wipe it off.

His grin stayed on his face until he entered the cool interior, the scent of animals, hay and dirt accosting him. Confusion reigned with children racing past him, several climbing on the stall doors and one swinging on a rope. The noise level skyrocketed the longer he stood there in the middle of the barn.

When Timothy rushed by him. Noah blocked the child's path. "Where are Peter and Jacob?"

Cara's son, his blond hair sticking straight up in places, shrugged. "Don't know."

If they were smart, they'd probably hightailed it out of here. Noah slowly turned in a full circle and noticed a group of children hovering at the other end of the line of stalls. He headed for the crowd.

When Noah peeked inside the last stall, he saw a pregnant chestnut mare lying on the hay while Peter and Jacob observed the delivery. Several of the kids pointed and exclaimed in anticipation when the front feet appeared with the foal's head between them.

Someone tapped Noah on the arm. He looked down.

"I can't see. Can you hold me up?" Lindsay clutched her stuffed bear to her. "I want to see the baby horse."

Although the little girl was six years old, she was small for her age and everyone towered over her. Noah scooped her up and lifted her high, setting her on his shoulders.

She grabbed his hair and leaned forward. "It's coming!"

The excitement in Lindsay's voice made Noah grin. "Have you ever seen an animal give birth?"

"No." She tugged on his hair as her grip tightened. "It's almost out."

At that moment the foal slipped completely from the mare and lay on the hay. The mother struggled to her feet and nuzzled her baby, which received some ahs from the children.

"She's licking it like Molly does me."

"Speaking of Molly, I understand Peter brought her into the barn."

"Yeah, Rusty took her for a walk. Peter said she'd been cooped up and needed to go potty." Lindsay bent toward Noah's ear and whispered, "He won't be happy he missed this."

From what he'd seen of the young boy, he wasn't

happy about much, but then Noah remembered all the anger he'd had as a child and could identify with Rusty. The boy could have a long road ahead without help.

Help I could give him.

That thought came unbidden into Noah's mind. He supposed after the children were settled in their new situation he could become a big brother to Rusty and try to mentor him.

Another tug on his hair centered his attention on the child perched on his shoulders. Who would help her? Cara? She would be perfect since it was obvious Lindsay liked her. She had clung to Cara at the hospital except when the girl had hugged Adam.

"The baby is getting milk. Look!"

Some of the children ahead of Noah wandered away now that the thrill was over. He moved closer, having to acknowledge that seeing the birth of the foal was exciting. He'd seen a few, but he still marveled at the wonder. Maybe there really was a God who made this all possible.

"There. I think the food is finally ready for consumption." Laura backed away from the picnic table laden with dishes. "Thanks for helping."

"It was fun and the guys had to take care of the kids while we did it." Hannah scanned the yard. "By the way, where are they?"

"The guys or the children?" Alice Henderson eased into a chair, parking her cane next to her on the deck.

Cara leaned against the wooden railing and watched the exchange between the three. Although she and Laura were good friends, she didn't know Hannah or Alice, Noah's foster mother, well. She'd heard stories about them from Laura, but it wasn't the same. They were a close-knit group who had bonded because of the children. She could remember as a teenager wanting to fit in with a certain clique and not being sure how to do it. The way she finally went had been totally wrong, throwing herself at one of the boys in that group. She was still paying for that mistake.

"Cara, you said Noah brought Molly. Where did they go?"

Laura's question pulled Cara away from the past and focused her on the present. "To the barn."

"Of course. That's where they usually end up." Hannah started down the steps with Laura right behind her.

When Cara stayed where she was, Laura glanced at her. "Want to come help round them up?"

"I'll stay and keep Alice company. I've seen you two in action. You can handle it. All you'll need to say is the food is on."

Hannah chuckled. "Yeah, and then get out of the way as they run out of the barn."

After the two women struck out across the yard, Alice patted the arm of a chair next to her. "Come sit. I haven't had much of a chance to talk to you, but I feel like I know you. Laura was always speaking of you. She looked forward to your e-mails."

Cara crossed the deck and settled into the place next to the older woman. "Laura told me about your illness and recovery."

"Not fast enough for me. I don't like being beholden to anyone, even my boys."

"Boys?"

"Peter, Jacob and Noah. They are like mother hens. Now that I'm living in the duplex next to Laura's aunt and not here anymore, one of them is stopping in to see me every day. And they've organized the other foster children I raised who still live in town to keep an eye on me. I had more privacy when I lived here."

"They love you. They don't want anything to happen to you."

"When it's my time, it's my time. I'll get to see Paul again. He's with the Lord, waiting for me." Alice smoothed out her flowered dress, setting her white handkerchief in her lap. "Enough about me. I'm boring. Tell me about you and Timothy. Such a sweet little boy."

"I'm the boring one," Cara said with a laugh.

"You've had some excitement in your life recently. Are you all right?"

"You mean what happened at the restaurant?"

"Yes, Peter said something to me when he picked me up."

"I wish I could say what happened was behind me, but I've got the feeling Jake and his friends are going to cause some problems for me."

"Oh, dear. We can't let that happen." Alice touched Cara's arm. "Noah won't let that happen."

"He may have no choice."

Alice gave Cara's arm a quick squeeze. "He's such a good man. He'll do what is necessary." The older woman peered toward the barn, observing the horde of children and adults exiting it. "I wish I didn't worry about him so much."

"Why?"

"I've never been able to bring him to the Lord. He still has anger from his childhood that gets in the way." Alice looked back at Cara. "I want to see him married and settled before I die. He needs a wife and children even though he doesn't think so."

The woman's probing gaze caused Cara to squirm in her chair. In that minute before the crowd reached the deck she felt as if she had been appraised and assessed. She wasn't sure she wanted to know what Alice had found. She remembered some of the things her husband used to say when they argued. The problem was, even now, she agreed with Tim. Her life was a lie. Her marriage had been a sham.

Cara forced a grin to her lips and shot to her feet. "I'd better get over there to help the children with their plates."

"Cara, will you do me favor and tell Noah to bring me a plate? He knows what I like to eat."

Cara peered back at Noah's foster mother and said, "Sure, but I can get you something to eat."

Alice fluttered her hand, her eyes twinkling. "Nonsense. It looks like you've got your work cut out for you. There are starving children wanting something to eat. Take care of them."

Cara found Noah standing behind Rusty. "Alice needs you to bring her a plate of food."

His gaze followed toward the direction she gestured. "I see she has her command post staked out."

"Noah! How can you say that?"

"Easy, from years of experience, and it was said with love and affection, but I know Alice Henderson. She's up to something when she begins to play the helpless one." He studied Cara for a long moment. "What did you two talk about?"

Heat rose into her cheeks. "I'd better get to work." She turned to disappear in the crowd of children.

Noah's hand on her arm stopped her escape. "Don't tell me. Let me guess. She talked about my lack of a wife and children."

The heat intensified, diffusing throughout her. "She does that a lot?"

"Lately that's her favorite subject ever since Jacob and Hannah got married." He grinned. "At least before that, she spread it around."

She patted his hand, still on her arm. "I'm sorry."

His laughter erupted from deep in his chest. The sound caused the children around him to stare up at him. Noah released his hold on her. "I'd better let you get to work."

Cara hurried to Laura, who finished spooning some potato salad onto a paper plate, then passed it to one of her twin boys. "What do you want me to do?"

Her friend stuck a large fork in her hand. "Serve the barbecue chicken, then pass me the plate."

By the women forming an assembly line the task went quickly. Cara dished up her last piece of meat fifteen minutes later then sank into a chair next to Laura with her own lunch ready to devour. "All this work has me hungry."

"It's been a busy day, and we haven't even gotten to the games yet."

Cara angled to face Laura. "Games! What games?"

"Oh, whatever the dear children come up with. My son is in charge."

"Which one? Sean, I hope."

Laura laughed. "I'm not crazy. No way would I let my twins be in charge of something like that. I can just picture what they'd have us do." She tapped her chin with her forefinger. "Let's see. How about a nice game of who will be the first one to break his leg jumping off the roof of the house?"

"And Timothy would be in the thick of it." Cara sensed someone sitting down in the chair on her other side. She glanced over and spied Noah.

"You and your son look alike, especially the eyes." Noah lifted a piece of chicken and took a bite.

Cara searched the crowd and found Timothy with Laura's twins sitting under a large oak tree in the back. She pointed to him. "In case you're color-blind, I have green eyes and he has brown ones."

"Not the color, the shape, the spacing. In fact, your mouths are the same, too." Noah lifted his iced tea and took a sip. "Timothy showed me where Peter and Jacob were hiding."

"Hiding?" Under Noah's intent scrutiny, the urge to squirm inundated her worse than when she had been talking with Alice.

"Well, not really. But I was thinking if they were smart that would be what they were doing."

"I thought you were involved in Stone's Refuge. Aren't you on the Henderson Foundation board?"

"Yes, I'm one of the founders of the refuge, and I do visit but I don't participate personally as much as Jacob and Peter. They are much more familiar with children than me. My participation is more along the lines of a monetary one."

"So children aren't your thing?"

He frowned. "I didn't say that exactly. I'm more comfortable around teens than young kids."

"I haven't had a chance to tell you what Children's Protective Services has come up with for Rusty, Lindsay and Adam." Laura leaned toward Noah and Cara and lowered her voice.

Noah tensed. "This doesn't sound good."

"It won't be the best solution and I foresee some problems, but there's nothing that can be done about it with the shortage of foster parents in Cimarron City."

"You weren't able to keep them together?" Cara curled her hand around the arm of the chair, knowing by Laura's sad look the answer.

"No. They tried. If I had room, I'd take them in. Our fourth house won't be finished for at least four or five months so we don't even have a place for them. Children's Protective Services has agreed to wait until Adam is out of the hospital in a few days before moving them." Laura tried to smile, but the corners of her mouth quivered. "The homes are supposed to be close to each other, maybe a mile or so between them."

"A mile! That might as well be across town." Noah's frown strengthened into a scowl that darkened his eyes. He bent closer to Laura and Cara, with his elbows on his knees and his hands gripped together. "There's got to be a way."

Her friend stared into Noah's angry face and said, "Then you take them in."

Chapter Five

"What?" Noah jerked back in his chair.

"Let's face it. You're the only one I know who has a huge house with plenty of room for three kids. In fact, they could get lost in your place. You probably wouldn't even know they were there." Laura scanned the yard as though counting her kids to see if they were all there.

"Yes, I would." The cords in his neck constricted, sending pain shooting through his shoulders and down his arms. "They make noise. When I'm home, I want peace and quiet."

"You're hardly home."

"Exactly. What kind of foster parent would that be?"

Laura scooted her chair closer, the sound of it scraping against the wooden deck grating down his spine. "I know when you agree to do something you put your all into it. These children would be blessed to have you as their role model. You already know Adam and I know you like him. I can see it. Adam can see it. So admit it."

"He stole from me."

"See how desperate he is."

Laura's statement punched Noah in the gut. Although he'd never stolen, he'd been that desperate when he was growing up, and no one had helped him until Alice and Paul had come along. They turned his life around and he owed them. Would taking the three children in for a few months be enough to pay them back for what they had done for him?

"Yeah, well, not as desperate as I would be if I had three kids running around my house." Any conviction he'd wanted to interject into his words somehow got lost as he continued to remember how the Hendersons had saved him.

Snapping her fingers, Peter's wife grinned. "I've got it. Hire someone to look after the children when you're working. Someone motherly. Someone who can be there when you have to work. They certainly need someone like that, especially Lindsay."

"Where in the world am I going to find someone motherly? The women I know, besides you and Hannah, aren't that type." Because that was the way he had wanted it. But he didn't need to tell Laura that. She knew he avoided any serious relationships. A shallow one was all he needed when he was looking for feminine companionship.

Laura's eyes widened, and her grin evolved into a full-fledged smile. "So you will think about it? That's great. I'm sure we can come up with someone who is good with children and can keep house. She could stay in the back bedroom off your kitchen. Wasn't it called a servant's quarters when you bought the house?"

"First, you want me to take in three children and now a kid-friendly housekeeper. My place is only so big." He started counting his bedrooms and had gotten to five when Laura waved both of her hands in excitement.

"I've got a better idea. How about your cottage behind the garage? It would be perfect. It was a guest house at one time."

"It still is. I just don't have guests. I like my privacy, Laura." Noah swung his attention to Cara, who sat next to her friend, listening to the exchange with a neutral expression. Maybe she could talk some sense into Laura because obviously what he was saying wasn't getting through. "Help me."

"A cottage? That certainly could be appealing to someone." Cara fidgeted in her chair.

No, I didn't mean help me that way, Noah wanted to shout.

"Cara, you're right." Laura angled toward her. "And you could be that someone. Noah's estate would be a wonderful place for your son. You're a great housekeeper." She shifted her attention back to him. "So you see, problem solved. Cara is interested in the job, so you've got the help you wanted." She jumped to her feet. "I'll leave you two to work the details out. I see Alexa bothering her little brother. I'd better put a stop to it before it gets out of hand."

Wide-eyed, Cara watched her friend scurry away.

Noah shook his head as Laura left. "I feel like I was struck by Hurricane Laura."

Cara chuckled, the sound a little shaky. "She's a force to be reckoned with."

"Now that's she gone, you don't have to pretend about the job."

"Pretend? Oh, you really weren't—I mean… You don't need a—"

"No, I needed help with Laura since you two are such good friends. She doesn't let an idea go when it takes root in her fertile mind."

Cara's laughter spiced the air. "That's my friend." Her full lips set in a pout, her forehead crinkled in question. "But I wasn't pretending. I'm better qualified to take care of your house than being a waitress. I know the waitress job is temporary and this one would be, too, but the prospect of having my own place is appealing."

"I'm crushed that you'd rather be a housekeeper than a waitress at *my* restaurant."

Those full lips he had no business staring at curved upward. "Aren't you forgetting that I want to be *your* housekeeper instead?"

"There is no housekeeping position. I have someone come in a couple of times a week to clean my house. That's all *I* need."

"But what about Adam, Rusty and Lindsay?"

The muscles in the back of his neck solidified into a rock. "There's bound to be someone better than me who can be a foster parent to them."

She gestured toward the people around them. "Where? Didn't you hear what Laura said? I don't see them lining up to take three children in. They'll split them up. This whole ordeal has been difficult on them and to have to be separated will be even more so."

Memories of how hard it had been for him and his sister to be separated washed over him. He looked around as though he hoped to see someone approaching offering to take them. All he saw were his friends and the children living at the refuge eating, laughing and talking as if they didn't have any problems. "You'd really rather be a housekeeper?"

She looked him square in the eye. "Yes. That's all I've really known. I'm good at it. At being the motherly type."

And that right there was why he would stay as far

away from her as possible. He'd just have to do it on his estate, because he couldn't say no to Laura's *gentle* suggestion for him to take the three in for a few months. In a way, he could return all those years given to him because of Alice and Paul. It would be just a measly three months or until they found someone legit to be the kids' foster parent. In the meantime he would do his own search for the right couple.

"Okay. You've got yourself a job, and when a place comes up that will take all three of them, I'll see if there's another job available at one of my restaurants, if you want. Deal?" He offered her his hand, which she shook.

"When do you think it will start?"

"It shouldn't take long for me to be approved since I have a working relationship with Children's Protective Service because of Stone's Refuge. They ran background checks on all of us involved with this place. I'd like you to be in place, so how about starting tomorrow?"

"You move fast when you set your mind on something."

"I've been accused of doing that a few times."

"Do you think Timothy will have to change schools? He's attending Washington Elementary."

"No, but Lindsay and Rusty will have to. Adam will be going to the same high school."

"That's not going to be easy for them."

Her green gaze, filled with such concern, snared him. "I know. But the good thing is that they should be in a permanent place when school starts next fall. And if they end up living in the fourth house here at the refuge, Washington will be their school."

"You don't think one couple will ever take them in?"

Noah searched the yard for Rusty and Lindsay. He

found Rusty talking to an older boy, new to the refuge. "No." Saying out loud what he knew would happen made it sound so final. He was too familiar with the system. The knot in his gut grew.

He started to return his attention to Cara when a shout erupted from Rusty, followed by the young boy tearing into the older one, his fists lashing out. Noah leaped up and raced toward the two kids. Noah arrived at the same time as Jacob who pulled the bigger child off Rusty and held him back while Noah caged his soon-to-be charge.

Rusty twisted and bucked. "Let me go."

The hostility in the nine-year-old flowed off him as Noah tried to avoid being kicked. "Not until you settle down and tell me what this is about."

"He's a liar." The words exploded from Rusty's mouth.

"You wish." The other boy glared at Rusty.

Noah motioned for Jacob to haul the kid he had away. When they were safely out of eyesight, Noah loosened his hold. "Now I'm going to let you go, and you and I are going to have a talk. Understand?"

A good minute later Rusty finally nodded, and Noah dropped his arms to his sides, fully expecting to have to chase down the boy when he tried to make a break for it. Surprisingly Rusty stood still, but the look in his eyes could have frozen Noah.

"What was he lying about?" What had he gotten himself into, Noah thought with near panic. The only refereeing he'd ever done was between two employees, two adults—or near adults in the case of his teenage workers.

"He said that Lindsay, Adam and me will be put in different homes. He heard Hannah talking about it."

"No, you won't be split up."

Rusty lifted his chin, pushing his shoulders back. "Where are we gonna live?"

"With me."

"That's the last box from the car," Noah said, setting it down on the floor in the living room of the cottage. "Are you sure this is okay?"

"It will be once I get it cleaned up. I'm glad Timothy is at school. Hopefully I'll have things under control before he gets ho—here." Cara rotated slowly around her new place.

Thank you, Lord, for providing a home for Timothy and me, even if it's only for a few months. It will give me time to figure out what I want to do with my life.

"If not, your son can help you."

She ran her finger along the counter in the small kitchen off the living area. "Not with the sweeping and dusting. Timothy has asthma. I have to be careful." She pointed to the wooden floor. "I'm glad there isn't any carpet in the cottage. That'll make it easier to keep clean for him. Dust sets him off."

"If I'd had time, I would have gotten a professional cleaning crew in here so you wouldn't have to spend your first day on the job cleaning this place."

"The state moved fast once they knew you'd take all three children."

He chuckled. "Fast? Don't you mean faster than a speeding bullet? I called the agency first thing this morning and talked with my friend. And here it's noon and you're moving in. Do you think they saw the sucker sticker on my forehead?"

"No, they snatched up the best situation for these three children, and I think the kids will come to realize that."

She would make it work because she owed Adam. He'd come to her rescue when she'd needed help in the parking lot and she would come to his.

He averted his head as if her compliment made him embarrassed. "Well, at least it's only temporary," he said in a quiet voice as though he needed to remind himself.

Silence descended for an uncomfortable moment. Glancing around, Cara shuffled from one foot to the other. What had caused this man to close himself off from people? He professed to be a loner and the brief tour of his house had reinforced that. She didn't know why he had bought such a big place to live in when it was obvious he used maybe four rooms in the whole mansion.

"You don't mind picking the kids up at school today?" she finally asked.

His gaze connected with hers, intense—and for a few seconds full of doubt. "No, especially since it will give you more time to get this cottage in order. I'll take Timothy with me to Stone's Refuge to get Rusty and Lindsay's belongings. I have a feeling once they hit my house you'll have your hands full."

The grin he gave her warmed her insides. "But not you?"

The smile widened. "I have dinner plans tonight."

With who? "Then you won't be home their first night?" She schooled her tone into a neutral one although disappointment flitted through her.

"I hadn't thought of it that way. I guess I could reschedule it if you think it's important."

"No, no." She fluttered her hand in the air, more to dismiss her regrets than his concerns. "We'll get along just fine."

Again quiet reigned. She moved toward a stack of

boxes with some of her cleaning supplies. She didn't understand her feelings when she certainly wasn't picturing anything with a man like Noah—handsome, worldly and not a Christian. "When will Adam be released from the hospital?"

"Tomorrow."

Was that relief in his voice?

"Then if Rusty and Lindsay play nice, I'll take them to see their brother," Cara said.

Opening the box, she studied its contents, keeping her attention trained away from him in case he could see her thoughts written on her face. She wasn't nearly as accomplished as he was in hiding her feelings.

"Ah, bribery. That ought to work."

"I call it negotiating. Like a contract you might have with someone. If you do this—" she presented her right hand, palm up "—you get this." She did the same with her left one.

"If you don't run away tonight, you get to see Adam?"

"Yes. Before long, you'll get the hang of it."

"Contracts and negotiating I can handle. That's right up my alley. Maybe this parenting thing isn't too hard."

She laughed so hard tears ran down her face. Swiping them away, she said, "Yeah, you keep thinking that. Did I tell you I have some swampland in Florida I'd like to sell to you?"

"I believe my new housekeeper is making fun of me."

Arching an eyebrow, she rummaged around in the box until she found her sponge. "You think?"

His amusement dimpled his cheeks and eased the growing tension between them. He swept his arm across his body and bent at the waist. "I bow before your expertise in child rearing. You will have to mentor me these next few months. Believe me, I'm in over my head and still wondering why in the world I agreed to do this."

"Because you saw a need and wanted to do something about it, even allowed yourself to be talked into something you didn't want to do."

"So you think you've got me figured out."

"Oh, no! I would never say that. My experience with men is very limited." She hurriedly dug around in the box until she found the cleaning liquid and started for the kitchen. "Now if I'm gonna get this place in ship shape order for my son, I need to get busy. If you stay, I'll put you to work."

"I think you're trying to get rid of me."

"Smart man."

"What if I tell you I have an hour before I need to be at work and I can help you until then?"

She stopped dead in her tracks and swung around to face him. "Really?" Her husband had always run in the other direction when she began cleaning.

"Actually, I'm kind of handy at it. Remember I have a chain of restaurants and have worked every position, including cleaning the restrooms."

"Well, in that case—" she walked back to the box and withdrew some more supplies, thrusting them toward him "—you can start with the bathroom."

"I'm gonna regret telling you that," he said with a chuckle, but he took the sponge and bottles and headed toward the back.

Cara set about tearing the kitchen apart, always conscious of Noah in the other room. Ten minutes into her task, he broke out whistling some song she wasn't familiar with. Before long she found herself whistling along with him as she scrubbed the sink.

Tim never would have helped her, not even taking care of his own study. But then she and her husband had never really been a team, and it had been her fault. Tim had been a good, Christian man.

Father, give me the strength to do what's right in raising my son alone. I know he misses his dad. Please help me fill that role in Timothy's life because I can never make the same mistake and marry for the wrong reasons. I—

"What's next?"

She gasped and jumped at Noah's deep voice cutting through her thoughts. Whirling around, her hand on her chest, she gripped the counter with the other one. "I didn't hear you."

"Sorry, I thought I sounded like a herd of wild mustangs."

She drew in several deep breaths before saying, "Don't you have to be at the restaurant?"

"I called and got Lisa to meet with the produce guy. I'm all yours till I have to pick the kids up at school."

I'm all yours stuck in her mind. She couldn't get past those words. Until she noticed him staring at her with a funny look as if he wasn't sure she was completely sane and was having seconds thoughts about her being his housekeeper. "You don't have to help. I know you're a busy man."

This was a side of Noah that surprised her—pleasantly. Then she remembered the danger in getting too emotionally involved with a man like Noah—a self-proclaimed bachelor who wanted to stay as far away from a family as he could.

"Who has rearranged his schedule so he could help. What do you want me to do next?"

Leave, so I can concentrate on my work. "Uh—how about one of the bedrooms?"

"Great. I'll tackle Timothy's. I'll let you clean your own."

As he left the room, he shot her that funny look again and she wheeled around to stare out the window over the sink. Embarrassment flushed her face; she could feel its heat. She shouldn't have taken this job. He wasn't going to be an easy man to ignore.

Lord, what was I thinking?

Noah stared at the beautiful woman across from him at the dining table, and all he could think about was Lindsay's big blue gaze watching him as he'd driven off tonight. The little girl had never said a word about him leaving, but he'd seen it all in her look. Disappointment had curved her mouth in a slight pout and saddened her eyes. Then he'd made a mistake and glanced at Cara, whose expression mirrored Lindsay's.

Two hours later he still wrestled with what to do. Normally he didn't second-guess his actions. He was always decisive until lately—since he'd met Cara.

"You aren't very hungry?" Jessica picked up her after dinner coffee and took a sip.

His plate sat in front of him while hers had been taken away ten minutes ago. He studied his half-eaten T-bone steak, probably cold by now, and tried to summon his usual healthy appetite. "I'm on a diet?"

She giggled. "You? You're the last person I would ever think would go on one. You must not eat those pizzas you sell." Her gaze slipped over what she could see of him above the table. "I'd give anything to eat like you and never gain an ounce. I have to watch everything I put in my mouth."

That was probably why she'd only had a salad and a glass of water with lemon for dinner at this four-star restaurant. They had been dating a few weeks and all he'd seen her eat was rabbit food. Jessica was tall and reed thin and could afford to add a few pounds—maybe ten or twenty.

"My agent called and I have a photo shoot in Dallas at the end of this week so I have to cancel our date Friday night." Her collagen-improved lips puckered in a pout that was not nearly as attractive as Lindsay's—or Cara's. "I'm so sorry. I won't be back into town until Saturday afternoon, late."

He waved his hand for the waiter. "That's okay. In fact, I need to cut this evening short. I took in three children today, and I should be at home." Was that him saying those words? There was a part of him that was startled to hear them come out of his mouth, and obviously by the surprise on Jessica's face she was, too.

"Whose children?"

"Some foster kids." When the waiter appeared, Noah said to him, "I'm through with my dinner. May I have the check please?"

"Was something wrong with the steak, Mr. Maxwell?" The man, dressed in a tuxedo, picked up the china plate.

"There was nothing wrong." *At least not with the food, just me.*

When the waiter left, Jessica folded her napkin on the table. "You take in foster children?"

"No, this is the first time."

"Oh, don't you have something to do with Stone's Refuge? I thought I read that in the newspaper."

"Yes." Her statements confirmed in his mind what he'd already known. They had shared little personal information on the five dates they had gone on before this one. He knew she was a model and beautiful, every feature picture-perfect as though a plastic surgeon had created his ideal woman.

"Oh, that must be…rewarding. I volunteered once at—"

Noah heard her as she spoke about her experience in high school. Then she launched into a description of the upcoming photo shoot she was doing. He watched her mouth move, forming her words, and he couldn't focus on what she was saying. He wanted to, but his thoughts kept wandering back to his house. Did Cara need his help with the kids? Had Rusty spoken yet or had he remained silent even through dinner? What did Timothy think of his new home?

The waiter placed a small silver tray on the table near him. He glanced at the bill and laid his credit card on top of it, hoping the man would hurry. Jessica continued to chatter about her day, hardly taking a breath between sentences.

Fortunately the waiter must have seen the distress in his eyes because he returned in two minutes. Noah quickly signed, giving the man a generous tip, then slipped his copy into his pocket and rose. As they walked out of the restaurant, he saw heads turn to watch them leave. Wherever Jessica went, men stared at her and she knew it.

Thirty minutes later Noah finally pulled into the long drive that led to his Tudor-style house. The darkened interior alarmed him. He parked in front and hurried toward the circular porch. They should have been home from the hospital by now. It was nearly ten. Aren't kids supposed to be in bed by eight or eight-thirty at the latest?

Their first night at his house and something was wrong. He should have been here.

He burst through the front entrance and rushed toward the great room, flipping on lights as he went. Voices from outside drifted to him. Cara appeared at the French doors with a smile on her face.

"You're home early," she said, stepping inside.

"Where are the kids?"

Her grin died. "They're okay. They're outside. I was showing them the constellations."

"In the dark?" He hadn't meant to sound so angry, but his heart still pounded a maddening pace.

"That's usually the best way to see them."

He took some calming breaths, and her vanilla scent saturated his senses, causing him to step back several feet as though distance between them would wipe her presence from his thoughts. He'd actually stared at Jessica's salad and thought of Cara's green eyes. Even the lemon in his date's water began to remind him of Cara's hair, which was really stretching his imagination since her color was more a platinum blonde.

She tilted her head to the side, considering him with those liquid green eyes that he couldn't forget. "Is there something wrong? Is that why you're home early?"

"Early? It doesn't take all night to eat dinner."

"But I thought you had a date. At least that was what I assumed." She blushed a nice shade of red.

He heard Lindsay say something to Rusty. "Aren't they supposed to be asleep by now?"

Cara glanced at her watch. "Yes. I didn't mean to keep them up this late, but when I start talking about the stars, I can get carried away."

"You like astronomy?"

"Yes. Several years ago I took a class at the local community college to learn more about the universe. After I finished the course, I was even more in awe of God's power and vision."

"In college I took several courses about astronomy. I even considered majoring in it, but I didn't in the end." A common interest, which he had given up in the pursuit of making money.

"Why not?" Cara asked.

"There isn't a great demand for astronomers in the job market."

"So did you just take it up as a hobby?"

"No, this is the first time I've thought about it in years." He looked around her and saw the three children in the doorway, watching them. "Time for bed. Tomorrow's a school day." He imagined—since he'd never had any experience as a child or adult—that many parents had been saying those very words all over America an hour ago.

Lindsay walked up to him. "Have you ever seen the Little Dipper?" Before he had a chance to answer her, she added, "I can show you it, if you want. Cara showed me."

"Sure." What was a minute or two if it helped the little girl go to bed?

Lindsay slipped her hand into his and pulled him toward the French doors. Rusty glared at the two of them, but Timothy followed them out onto the deck.

She stood at the railing and pointed skyward. "See, it starts there." She drew her finger down and around. "That's the North Star. Cara said that people have used that star to guide them home. I'm gonna show Adam when he comes tomorrow so he won't get lost."

Noah's throat thickened. Had his little sister ever looked up at the stars and thought about him and home?

Now that she was an adult, why hadn't she ever returned to Cimarron City? Was she even alive? A mantle of loneliness cloaked him. Usually he wore it with no problem, but today…

"That's a good idea, Lindsay. Adam will appreciate that," Cara said as she came to the little girl's side.

Her presence yanked him back to the here and now. "Thanks, Lindsay." He turned away and strode back into the house, shoving the past down into the dark recesses of his heart where it belonged. "Now, everyone to bed."

No one moved.

He glanced from Lindsay to Rusty, then in desperation to Cara, silently sending her an SOS.

Cara put her hand on the little girl's shoulder. "Remember where we put your things? That's where you'll be sleeping. Lindsay, I'll help you get ready before Timothy and I leave. Show me the way."

"You don't remember?" the little girl asked.

"If you help me, we can find it." Cara and Lindsay started for the stairs with Timothy trailing behind them.

Noah faced Rusty. "That includes you."

Rusty crossed his arms. "I'm not tired."

At least the boy was talking although his statement wasn't what Noah wanted to hear. "Then lie in bed until you get sleepy."

"At home I never went to bed at the same time as Lindsay. She's a baby. I'm not." The nine-year-old lifted his chin in challenge.

"This is a new house, new rules." Did he sound stern enough?

The boy's eyes narrowed. "Says who?"

Noah pointed to himself. "Me. In case you haven't noticed, I'm bigger than you."

For a second Rusty's eyes grew round before his defiant look returned.

Great! I'm using terror tactics on a child. "But I'm not going to use that to prove my point. If you want to stay down here and sleep, go ahead. I'm tired and after your sister goes to sleep, I'm going to bed. Good night."

The area between Noah's shoulder blades tingled as he strolled toward the circular staircase, switching off most of the lights as he went. At the bottom he glanced back and saw Rusty quickly turn away.

On the second floor, Noah made his way to Lindsay's bedroom and paused in her doorway. Cara tucked the little girl in and kissed her forehead, murmuring good-night.

He advanced inside. "Please wait," he whispered as Cara passed him on her way to the hallway.

"See you tomorrow, Timothy." Lindsay snuggled down under the covers.

"Night." The boy's face reddened, and he hurried after his mother.

Yawning, Lindsay looked up at him. "Timothy and some of the other kids at the refuge showed us around the school today."

He sat on the bed, feeling awkward. "Do you like your new teacher?"

"She's nice. She has a puppy at home and two cats."

"You like animals?"

"Yes!" she said as though there should be no doubt.

Duh, what kid didn't! He would need to work on his repartee where kids were concerned. "I have some ducks on my pond."

"You do? Can I see them tomorrow?"

"Sure. The faster you go to sleep, the faster tomorrow will get here."

She shot up and threw her arms around his neck, kissing him on the cheek. "Good night." Her baby-soft cheek brushed against his. Then she settled back onto the bed and closed her eyes.

Her sudden action took him by surprise. Her kiss wormed its way into his heart.

When he didn't move for a full ten seconds, one of her eyes opened halfway. "You okay?"

He blinked and rose. "Yes. I was just making sure you were going to sleep."

Instead of saying anything, she yawned again and hugged her pillow. Noah tiptoed out of the room, dimming the light.

"You can turn it off. I'm not afraid of the dark," Lindsay said from beneath the covers.

He did but left the door open. Striding down the hall, he paused by Cara who waited at the top of the stairs. "Rusty refused to come upstairs. I told him that he could sleep down there, that I was going to bed."

"Do you want me to say anything to him?"

"No, but set the alarm before you leave. I'll see you tomorrow morning."

She descended two steps, stopped and peered back at him. "You did a good thing today. Rusty will realize you aren't the enemy. I'll be over to fix breakfast."

The thought of someone preparing him breakfast brought a smile to his mouth and lightened his mood, in spite of the thought of Rusty downstairs, probably still standing in the very same spot.

When Noah climbed into bed a few minutes later, sleep grabbed him and held him tightly…until a high-pitched noise pierced his dreamworld, and he bolted upright. The house alarm blared.

Chapter Six

Cara leaped from her bed, her heart beating so fast that her head spun from the sudden movement. Snatching up her terry robe, she stuffed her feet into her slippers then raced toward the front door and yanked it open. The shrill of the alarm shattered the quiet; the flood of outside lights illuminated every dark crevice around Noah's mansion, as though the sun had risen in the night.

"Mom, what's going on?" Timothy came up behind her, rubbing his eyes.

"I don't know. Noah's alarm is going off." What to do? Call him? The police? Hide? Go to the house and see if she could help?

Before she formulated a plan, the alarm stopped and silence blessedly ruled. Then the French doors opened, and Noah, dressed in jeans and a shirt he was buttoning, strode outside and stood on the deck. He searched the back area, his gaze ending its sweep when he saw her.

She belted her thick robe against the chill. "Timothy, stay right here. Let me see what the problem is. It was probably just a false alarm."

Cara skirted the pool and cabana and stopped a few yards from the deck off the great room, looking up the couple of feet to where Noah was. "What happened?"

"We have two missing children. Since I have a high fence around the property and the gate is locked, they're probably still nearby."

"I'll get dressed and help you search. It's cold. I don't want them out here too long."

"I'll get a jacket and shoes and meet you back here in a few minutes."

When she entered the cottage, Timothy hugged her. "I was scared when I heard that noise and then you weren't in your room."

She knelt in front of him. "Everything's all right. Rusty and Lindsay have run away again."

"Why? This place is so neat. There's a heated pool, a game room, a pond."

"They aren't happy. Their life is changing so much and they're afraid."

"Oh, like me."

"Are you afraid now?"

Timothy nodded. "I don't know anyone but you, Laura and her kids." Tears welled in his eyes. "I miss Daddy."

Cara rubbed her hands up and down his arms, remembering how excited he had been when they'd first left St. Louis. He had wanted to see his two friends so badly, but now reality was setting in for her son. "I know, sweetie. But he's with Jesus."

"I want him here with me."

She embraced her son. "Everything is different now, but give it a couple of months. You'll have new friends and as you said this place is neat."

When Timothy pulled back, he yawned. "Yeah, and I like visiting the barn at the farm."

"Remember Noah said something about ducks that live at his pond."

"Maybe they'll have babies."

Cara rose. "I'm going to help search for Rusty and Lindsay. Why don't you go back to sleep?"

"I'm not—" A big yawn interrupted him.

"You aren't tired?"

"Okay, maybe I am." Timothy shuffled toward his room.

Cara tucked him back into bed, kissed him good-night for the second time, then hurried to get dressed. Three minutes later she flew from the cottage and ran toward the pool area.

Switching off the cabana's light, Noah exited it. "They aren't in there or around here."

"Where do you think we should look first?"

Noah handed her a large flashlight. "The pond and gazebo. And remind me to sign both of the kids up for swimming lessons immediately. With all this water around here, I want to make sure they know how to swim well."

"I can teach them. The pool is heated and we can start lessons tomorrow after school. The days are pretty warm."

He shot her an assessing look. "I'm continually amazed at all your abilities."

"Except I have few marketable skills."

"It's all in how you look at it. I find right now your skills are invaluable to me."

Warmed by his compliment, Cara stepped out of the pool of floodlights into the darkness beyond. The half-moon brightened the night some, but there were a lot of places a child could hide in the expanse of yard that encompassed Noah's estate.

At the white gazebo near the pond, Noah flipped on the lights that illumined its immediate surroundings. "I was so hoping they were lying on the lounge chairs in here sleeping."

"As you said, we'll find them. They can't be too far."

Noah gestured with his flashlight. "I'll go around the pond this way and you go that way."

Cara circled the body of water and met Noah on the opposite side. "Anywhere else that comes to mind?"

"It'll take a while, but I think we should next walk the perimeter by the fence. There are a couple of places where I could see Rusty trying to climb a tree to get over."

The strain in his voice reflected her own inner turmoil. "Did you notice any of their things gone?"

"Lindsay's bear. They took a coat and shoes, too."

"Good. I was worried they would get cold."

"Maybe if they had gotten cold, they would be back at the house."

"Normally I would say yes, but Rusty is a hard case to crack."

Noah started for the back of the property behind the pond. "Sadly he reminds me of myself."

"Why sadly?"

"Because the road ahead won't be an easy one for him if he continues on the same path."

"First hand knowledge?"

"Most definitely." Noah halted by a large oak tree next to the eight-foot chain-link fence and shone his light up into the branches. "Nothing."

Cara strode east, inspecting the area around the fence while Noah checked the yard toward the house. When they reached an elm tree, again he examined it from bottom to top.

"I used to love to climb trees. There was an elm tree that I built a fort in. It really was just a few old boards I found, but it was my special place. That's where I would hide when I needed to."

"Hide? From who?"

Noah began walking again. "My father."

"There were times I felt like that, too. My father wouldn't let me do what other kids did. He was always afraid something bad would happen to me. I promised myself when I had a child, I wouldn't be overprotective." When Noah didn't say anything, she glanced over at him.

He slowed, his jaw set in a hard line. "I didn't have to worry about that with my dad. He didn't care what Whitney and I did." Waves of tension flowed off Noah.

Cara held her breath while she waited for Noah to continue speaking.

"He was mean when he wasn't drinking and he was twice as mean when he was." The matter-of-fact way he spoke didn't totally cover up the pain in his voice.

Cara's heart tore into pieces. "Where was your mom?"

Noah shrugged, picking up his pace. "Right after Whitney was born, she left. Dad got worse after that."

"Oh, Noah, I'm so sorry." The words weren't enough to express her horror and feelings concerning child abuse.

"You have nothing to be sorry about. That's in the past. I don't think about it."

"But—"

"Here's the other elm tree I have," he cut in, although they were still ten yards away. "If I was going to climb a tree to try and get over this fence, it would be one of the elms." Noah paused under it and swung his light upward.

Cara heard a whimpering sound from behind a large bush nearby. She started for it when Noah shouted, "Rusty, I know you're up there. Come on down."

The whimpering evolved into sobbing, and Cara hurried forward. "Lindsay?"

The little girl, clutching her bear, launched herself at Cara. "I didn't want to leave, but Rusty said we had to." Although she had on a jacket, she trembled against Cara.

"Rusty, I'm not angry. I know you want to go back home, but someone else is moving in tomorrow afternoon." Noah peered over his shoulder at Cara and Lindsay. "Is she okay?"

"Yes, just cold." Cara hugged the child to her to help warm her shivering body.

"It's our home. No one has the right to move in."

"The landlord told me he was getting ready to evict your family. The rent hasn't been paid in nearly three months."

Rusty came down one limb. "What about our stuff?"

"I'm going over tomorrow morning to load the rest of it up and bring it here."

Lindsay broke away from Cara and covered the few feet to Noah. She tapped him on the back. "What about Molly? Can we have her here?"

"I don't—"

"Please. I miss Molly."

Keeping the light trained on the elm, Noah turned slightly toward the little girl. "You don't think she would be happier at the farm with the other animals?"

Lindsay shook her head. "She misses us. We saved her."

"You did?"

"She was whining because she was all alone. Adam brought her home to me and I took care of her. Please."

Noah raked his hand through his hair and glanced toward Cara, a question in his gaze. Cara nodded.

He swung back around. "Rusty, if you come down right now, I'll pick Molly up tomorrow, too, and bring her here to live."

When the boy didn't say anything, Lindsay walked to the base of the tree and placed her hand on her waist. "You better get down here. I want Molly."

Cara nearly laughed at the girl's stern voice. But she noticed that her brother started his descent, one slow branch at a time.

She planted herself next to Noah. "Not bad negotiating."

A grin inched across his face. "I told you that was something I could handle."

"I do want to warn you there is more to raising children than negotiating with them. You'll need to give them some of your time."

"A home isn't enough?"

Cara started to say no when she saw the humor dancing in his eyes.

"Gotcha." He chuckled. "My parents might not have been good role models, but Alice and Paul were. Not to mention Laura and Peter, and Hannah and Jacob. They're all great with their children."

"Good, because you'll need those examples."

Rusty hopped the remaining few feet to the ground and stood next to his sister, taking her hand. "I made Lindsay come with me. She didn't want to. Don't be mad at her."

Noah wheeled around and began walking toward the house. "I'm not mad at either of you."

Rusty trailed behind a few feet. "You aren't?" Puzzlement marked his expression.

Cara strode next to Lindsay and used her flashlight to brighten their path. "No, we aren't, but I do think we need to talk about this when we get inside."

Silence accompanied the trek back to the house. While Noah took Rusty and Lindsay to his place, Cara checked on Timothy to make sure he was still sleeping, then she made her way to the deck and entered through the French doors.

Rusty, with Lindsay plastered against him, her teeth clattering, sat on the brown leather couch in the great room, staring at the floor. Noah paced in front of them.

"I'm making some hot chocolate." Cara retrieved a blanket from the closet and draped it over Lindsay's shoulders then headed for the kitchen.

Ten minutes later she entered the great room, carrying a tray with four mugs on it. She passed the drinks to everyone and said, "Please sit, Noah. You're making me nervous."

He plopped down in a matching leather chair across from the couch and sipped his drink. Cara eased into the other one and faced the children.

"I want to make it clear, Rusty, that there isn't any place better for you and your brother and sister than here." Cara let that sink in for a few seconds before continuing. "You absolutely can't live by yourselves. Adam can't go to school and support you all."

Rusty thrust back his shoulders. "I can get a paper route to help."

"No, that still wouldn't be enough, and living on the streets isn't an option. Would you want Lindsay exposed to that kind of life? It isn't safe, especially for children." Cara cradled the warm mug in her cold hands. "I need you to promise you won't try to run away again."

Rusty frowned.

Lindsay looked up from drinking her hot chocolate, a light brown mustache over her upper lip. "I promise. This will be a good place for Molly. She'll be able to run around. Please, Rusty, I don't want to leave. It's cold out there."

"Not for long. Summer will be here soon," the boy mumbled between sips of his beverage. "We would have gotten away if it wasn't for that alarm. I thought they were for keeping people out, not in. I ain't living in a prison."

Noah leaned forward, resting his elbows on his thighs. "If you give me your promise, I'll teach you the code to shut the alarm off. I set it at night to alert me if anyone is trying to get into the house."

Chewing on his bottom lip, Rusty stared at Noah. "Okay."

"Then when you go up to bed, I'll demonstrate how to set the alarm and turn it off."

The boy's eyes narrowed. "What if I don't want to sleep in that bedroom?"

"I have three more, all downstairs. If you want to choose one of them, that's fine by me. I just thought you would want to be upstairs with Lindsay and Adam."

The little girl clutched her brother's arm. "I want you upstairs with me."

Rusty shifted his attention to his sister. "Okay, but I don't like the room."

Noah rose. "Sleep in it tonight and we'll talk tomorrow about it. I think we should all go to bed."

Cara came to her feet and presented the tray to each one to put their mugs on. "I'll wash up, set the alarm and leave."

Lindsay walked to Cara. "Please put me in bed."

The pleading in the child's voice and eyes melted Cara's heart. She'd always wanted a little girl, too. She was afraid she was going to become too attached to the children. What would happen when they left for a more permanent foster home?

Upstairs she repeated tucking Lindsay into bed and kissing her goodnight. When she came out into the hall, Noah waited for her by the stairs.

"Rusty in bed?" Cara asked, her expression neutral.

"Yes, and quickly falling asleep."

She started down the steps. When Noah followed, she said, "You don't have to come downstairs. I'll lock up after I clean up the mugs."

"Leave them. You need to get your sleep, too. I'll walk you to the cottage."

"You don't have—"

He silenced her with a finger to her lips. "I want to. I appreciate your help tonight." Opening the French doors, he waited for her to go ahead of him. "How was Timothy when you checked on him?"

"Dead to the world. He's never been a light sleeper. He slept through the night starting at three months and the only time he gets up is when he's sick—or a house alarm goes off in the middle of the night."

"Sorry about that."

"No, it was a good thing." She strode past the pool. "We'll start the swimming lessons tomorrow afternoon. It will be nice for Timothy to practice, too."

At the cottage door she turned to thank him and caught his intense scrutiny. "Is something else wrong?"

He shook his head. "You're so different from most of the women I know—well, except for Laura, Hannah and Alice."

She thought of how she must look with no makeup on, her hair barely combed and in her "around the house" clothes that were comfortable but didn't conceal that extra ten pounds she'd gained since Tim's death. Then she pictured the women she'd heard Noah had dated—flawless beauties with not an extra ounce of fat. *My worth is what's inside,* she told herself while she grappled with what to say to him.

"I'm in good company with Laura, Hannah and Alice."

He smiled. "They are exceptional women."

He'd come close to giving her another compliment, two in one day. The realization shivered through her. Then another insight took her by surprise: she wanted to appeal to him in a feminine way. She hadn't felt that way in years.

"Thank you for your help." He inched closer.

"Just part of my job." She held her ground although she could smell his fresh clean scent that reminded her of the spring air enveloping them.

"Not at midnight."

"Didn't you realize being a parent isn't a nine-to-five job?"

"You mean it's 24/7?"

"Yeah."

"So I can expect to be awakened out of a sound sleep from time to time?"

"Probably, but at least they aren't infants or my answer would be definitely."

"I guess I'd better count my blessings."

"You are blessed."

His eyes widened. "I hadn't thought of my life as being blessed, but you're right. I have good friends and make a good living. I should be content."

"But you aren't?"

He took her hand and squeezed gently. "Good night, Cara. I'll see you in the morning." Then he disappeared into the night with that unreadable expression on his face.

A minute later the lights from the house revealed Noah mounting the stairs up to the deck before vanishing inside.

I should be content. Those words echoed through her mind. He wasn't. But then neither was she. Two troubled souls searching for something. At least she had the Lord to help guide her way. He didn't.

Is that why I'm here? To be his guide to You.

"You all did great! Before long you'll be swimming like fish." Cara sat next to Lindsay on the walk-in pool step and faced the two boys standing up in the shallow end.

"Can we stay in a while longer, Mom?"

"Sure. Just stay down at this end."

Timothy and Rusty headed to the other side while Lindsay jumped up and waved.

"Adam! I can float! Wanna see?"

Cara didn't have to turn to know that Noah was with Adam. She could feel his gaze on her, intense, the way it was the night before. Suddenly she remembered what she was wearing—a one-piece bathing suit that didn't hide those extra ten pounds. Could she stay in the pool until he left? Already her fingers were wrinkled.

"Let's see, Lindy." Using crutches, Adam lumbered toward a chaise lounge and eased down on it.

"Will you watch, too?" Lindsay asked Noah.

For a second so brief Cara almost missed it, astonishment widened Noah's eyes before he nodded.

Cara glimpsed nervousness in the little girl's gaze

although she tried to present a brave front to her brother. Lindsay hadn't come into the pool until Rusty and Timothy had been in for twenty minutes working on their swimming. Finally she'd allowed Cara to hold her in the water, then she attempted to float so long as Cara kept her arms under her.

"Do you want me to keep my arms under you?" Cara asked, moving close to the child.

Lindsay scooted down to the bottom step. "No, I think I can do this by myself. I'm a big girl now." The last was said in a whisper as though she had to remind herself of that. "But you can be right next to me," she added as she glided a foot from the stairs. "Just in case."

"I won't let anything happen to you," Cara said in such a low voice that Lindsay was the only one who could hear.

Noah stood at the edge of the pool near the boys. His gaze connected with Cara's before it settled on Lindsay. "I brought Molly."

The little girl beamed. "Where is she?"

"Exploring her new yard."

Fear darkened the Lindsay's eyes. "She can't run away, can she?"

"No, the gate is closed. She's safe. Show us how you can float."

Lindsay lay back in the water, looking up at the sky, her arms limp at her sides. She held the position for twenty seconds then began to sink. Quickly she put her feet on the bottom of the only area she could stand up in.

"See. Cara is gonna teach me to float with my face in the water next."

"By summer, sis, you're gonna be a pro," Adam said.

"Mom, me and Rusty want to sit in the hot tub." Timothy pointed toward the spa connected to the pool.

"It's okay with me if Noah is okay with it." Cara looked toward the man still near the boys at the edge.

"It's fine. If I didn't have so much to do, I'd join y'all swimming. Today's been beautiful and warm for the end of March."

Cara saw Molly charge around the side of the house and make a beeline for them. She started to say something about the big puppy, but the words didn't form fast enough to warn Noah that the dog was coming straight at him. He turned at the same second Molly propelled herself against him, her tail wagging.

Noah lost his balance and plunged into the water. A huge splash soaked Adam and the boys, still in the pool. Giggles erupted from the children as Noah came up spluttering. Wet hair covered his eyes. He swiped it back and glared at Molly. She must have taken it as an invitation because she leaped into the water and padded toward Noah.

"She likes you." Cara tried to contain her laughter, but seeing him drenched was funny. She covered her mouth.

"Not for long if I get my hands on her." His glare found the puppy biting at the water she was churning in front of her.

"You said you wanted to go swimming. She must have heard you." Cara's laughter burst forth, and she plopped down on the middle step, next to Lindsay.

"Molly, come here," the little girl said, holding out her arms for her pet.

The puppy changed course, barely missing Noah's grasp, and swam toward Lindsay. Cara scooped her up and hugged Molly. The dog licked her.

Noah waded toward the stairs. Lindsay jumped to her feet and hurried out of the pool with Molly following. The puppy stopped and shook the water off her, beads of liquid pelting Cara in the face.

Both Rusty and Timothy raced toward the steps and rushed up them before Noah planted himself in front of Cara, keeping his gaze trained on the dog who was greeting the boys with licks. Cara pressed her lips together to stop from laughing, but the sight of Noah in a light blue long-sleeved dress shirt and navy-blue slacks was priceless.

"Go ahead. Laugh. I know you want to." Noah sat next to her, water lapping at his chest. "My three-hundred-dollar shoes are probably ruined."

She sobered. "Three hundred dollars! Oh, my, I'm sorry. You shouldn't have changed after cleaning out the kids' house."

"I had to go by the Children's Protective Services office before picking up Adam. The way I looked would have made them reconsider their decision to let me have them."

Rusty, Timothy and Lindsay kept looking back at them as they walked toward the spa. Their giggles sprinkled the air.

"I always like to be the entertainment," Noah grumbled. "I knew there was a reason I never had pets."

"You've never had a pet, ever?"

"No, I work long hours and didn't think it was fair if I was never here."

"You didn't while you were a child?"

"My dad wouldn't let me. They cost money he wanted to spend on liquor."

"I'm sorry."

"Don't be. I was fine without having one."

She slanted a glance toward him, trying to read the

emotion behind the nonchalant response. A bland expression greeted her. "Were you?"

He pinned her with a penetrating gaze. "It took all my energy to protect my sister from my father. He would have used the pet against me."

She touched his arm. The picture he painted of his childhood broke Cara's heart. Her parents might have been overprotective, but she'd always known they loved her.

Noah peered down at her hand, then jerked to his feet and sloshed out of the pool, crossing to the house. "I don't want your pity." The door slamming reverberated through the air.

It hadn't been pity, but compassion. Still she wasn't sure Noah had had much of that in his life.

Cara gave the kids ten more minutes then said, "Time to get out. I need to prepare dinner."

"Can't we stay in, Mom?"

"I can't fix the food and watch you all, too."

"Adam can." Rusty popped up over the ledge of the spa.

Cara waved her hand toward the teen whose eyes were closed as he lounged in the chair. "I don't think so. He's in a cast. Besides, I want your homework done before dinner, so out. Now."

Grumbles followed her command, but first Lindsay, and then the boys exited the spa. Rusty and Lindsay headed for the deck. Timothy waited for her.

Cara walked by Adam and started to wake him up but decided to let him sleep until she had changed. Strolling next to her son, she made her way to the cottage.

At the door Timothy looked up at her. "I like Rusty."

"That's good."

"Can we play video games after dinner?"

"Only if your homework is totally finished."

"Great. I don't have much." Her son raced toward his bedroom, a huge grin on his face.

She scanned the living area, feeling content with the direction her life was going for the first time in years. Her attachment to Lindsay, Rusty and Adam growing, she didn't want them to go to a new foster home.

Was there any way she could take the children in and be their foster mother? The answer that came to mind wasn't the one she wanted to hear. She was having trouble taking care of herself and Timothy so how could she take on three more.

She trudged to the bathroom and quickly showered and dressed. "Timothy, we need to go up to the main house."

"Be there in a sec."

Her son's idea of a second usually meant ten minutes. She started for his room when a pounding at the front door drew her around. She hurried toward it.

When she opened it, Rusty was shifting from one foot to the other. "Come quick. Molly is acting strange."

Chapter Seven

"What's wrong with Molly?" Lindsay cried.

Noah stroked the puppy that trembled and drooled. "I think she's having a seizure or something like that. Has she ever done this?"

The little girl shook her head, tears streaking down her cheeks.

Noah looked around. "Where did Rusty go?"

"He went to get Cara," Lindsay said.

"Why?" Noah asked.

"She's had several dogs as pets."

And I haven't. His lack of experience with pets hadn't bothered him until now. He didn't know what to do.

The puppy stirred, the quivering subsiding. Lindsay rubbed her hand over Molly.

"Maybe she drank too much chlorinated water," Noah said.

The fear in Lindsay's eyes scared him. They'd had too much change in the past few days.

God, if You're listening, please don't let anything happen to Molly. Not for me, but for Lindsay. She loves the puppy.

The French doors opened, and Cara ran into the great room. Kneeling next to him, she asked, "What happened?"

"I don't know." Noah moved back a little to allow Cara more room. "I came downstairs and found her like this. She's been shaking and drooling for the past ten minutes at least."

"Did she get into anything?" Cara looked around, her gaze stopping. She rose and walked toward the kitchen. "I think I know what it was." She turned around a plate with a chocolate cake on it.

The dessert was missing several large chunks from one side.

"I'll call Roman and see what he thinks we should do." Noah headed for the phone.

"I had a dog get into some chocolate candy once, eating wrapper and all. I had to take mine to the vet. She's having muscle spasms."

With round eyes, Lindsay paled. "Will she die?"

"Hopefully Molly will be fine, but we'll need to watch her carefully from now on and make sure she doesn't get hold of any more chocolate. It's not good for pets." Returning to the puppy, Cara ran her hand along her flank. "You'll be okay, Molly."

Lindsay took what Cara said and murmured it over and over to her pet.

Roman answered on the third ring, and Noah explained what happened. When he hung up, he announced, "The vet Roman works for can see Molly right now. Rusty, go get Adam. He'll watch y'all while Cara and I take her to the doctor." He looked toward Cara. "Will you drive while I carry her and hold her?"

"Yeah, I'll go get my purse and keys then pull my car around front."

Adam hobbled into the room with Rusty trailing him. "What's going on?" the teen asked, his voice groggy as if he wasn't totally awake.

"I need to take Molly to the vet. Will you watch the children while we're gone?" Noah asked, squatting again next to the puppy.

Quickly covering his concern, Adam struggled to the coach and sat, laying his crutches down next to him. "Sure."

"I want to go, Noah. Please." Lindsay's eyes teared up, her lower lip sticking out.

"Fine. Roman said we might have to leave Molly overnight at the vet."

"I want to go," Rusty chimed in.

"Me, too." Timothy walked over to Rusty.

"Hey, you two. I don't want to stay home by myself. I thought we could play a video game." Adam picked up his crutches and began to rise. "Molly doesn't need all you guys tagging along."

"Okay," Rusty mumbled and scuffled toward the game room.

Timothy held one of Adam's crutches while the teen used the other to help him stand. Then Cara's son raced after Rusty.

Adam slowly made his way, pausing near Noah. "I figured you didn't need two more asking a zillion questions."

Probably not a bad idea since he wasn't too sure of the answers if it had to do with pets. Noah lifted the fifty-pound puppy into his arms. "Lindsay, will you open the front door?" Feeling Molly still quivering against him, he added, "We better get going."

As Lindsay walked toward the foyer, Adam paused at

the entrance into the game room. "Hey, Lindy. Noah will take care of everything. Molly is in good hands."

The teen's words both alarmed and pleased Noah. By the time he finished struggling to get the puppy into the car, however, his overriding thought was what would he do if something did happen to Molly and he let Lindsay down.

Two hours later Noah held the French doors open so Cara, Lindsay and Molly could go inside. He trudged in after them, exhausted from the brief exertion of emotional energy with Molly. The incident with the cake only reinforced the reason he didn't have a pet. What if she had died? He shook that thought from his mind and walked toward the kitchen.

In the great room Lindsay threw her arms around Molly and kissed her. "I'm so glad you're here and you didn't have to stay at the vet." As Adam entered, she rushed up to him and hugged him. "We're all together now."

Cara strode to the counter where the ruined cake still sat and dumped it into the trash. "Dinner in twenty minutes."

"Dinner? I thought you had to cook it." Noah got a whiff of something cooking and remembered he had smelled that earlier, right before Lindsay screamed because Molly was shaking so bad.

Cara stuck a foil-wrapped object into the oven. "I slaved away before the kids came home from school." She gestured toward the counter. "I have stew cooking in the Crock-Pot. We'll have that and French bread. I don't usually have dessert, but I baked the cake this morning as a welcome home surprise for Adam. I still have some ice cream, but that's all in the way of a sweet. I wanted to make this first dinner special."

Noah peered toward the teen interacting with his siblings. "Somehow I don't think that will matter."

Cara looked where he had. "Yeah, they're just happy to be together."

"You know on the ride here Adam asked my forgiveness for stealing from me. I told him he had it, but he was fired."

"Fired?"

"I run a business. How long do you think I would be in business if people thought it was okay to steal from me?"

"You can't give him a second chance?"

"No. I want Adam to devote his time to his studies. I found out from the school the last few months his grades have been going down. He doesn't have to work while he is staying with me." Noah lifted the top of the pot and drew in a deep breath of the wonderful aroma of meat, onions, carrots and potatoes, spiced with different herbs. His stomach rumbled. "I'm hungry."

She took the lid and replaced it. "And you will have to wait until it is ready. Go make yourself useful and set the table in the dining room."

He frowned. "I thought I was the employer."

Cara withdrew the plates from the cabinet and thrust the stack into his hands. "That doesn't mean you can't pitch in."

Noah quickly set the table while Cara made the kids go wash up, then she dished the food into a large bowl. The aroma continued to tease his hunger pangs. By the time he sat and served himself, he could hardly wait to dig into the food.

He picked up his fork and started to use it when Cara said, "Timothy, do you want to say the prayer?"

The eight-year-old bowed his head and folded his hands together in front of him. The others followed suit. Noah's gaze swept from one to the other. He reluctantly put his fork down and stared at his plate. This reminded him of the time he lived with Alice and Paul. Memories, not tainted with hatred, flooded him with a pleasant feeling.

"Lord, thank you for making Molly better. Please bless this food. Amen."

Amen, Noah repeated in his mind, especially for Molly.

When he looked up, he caught sight of Cara watching him. She was a lot like Alice. That in itself made him wary. He had to keep his distance. She was dangerous to the way he saw his life. If he needed no one, then no one would disappoint him and hurt him. And in return, he wouldn't disappoint and hurt that person. So far there had been nothing to change his mind from the course he had chosen for himself as a teenager.

"I'm glad you could come." Noah grasped the handle and opened the door. "This is new territory for me."

"So you were never in trouble while in school?" Cara walked past Noah into Rusty's classroom.

"I could say I was a model student, but we both know that would be a lie. I never thought I would take part in a parent conference."

His casual touch at the small of her back focused Cara's attention on the man beside her, not the older woman sitting at the teacher's desk. She didn't think she would ever get over her reaction to his nearness. She'd been his housekeeper for almost two weeks and she knew every time he entered a room even when she hadn't heard or seen him come in. When he was home, the place came alive, everyone but Rusty responding to his electrifying presence as though he charged the air with his energy. Even Adam wasn't too upset about being fired, because he was able to study more and bring his grades up.

Cara slowed her pace, finally taking in Rusty's teacher, her face sculpted in a frown, her body rigid. "I don't think she's too happy."

"She definitely didn't call this meeting to tell us how great Rusty was adjusting to his new school." His gaze swept the area. "Where is he? I know I'm new at this, but shouldn't he be here?"

"It might be a good thing he isn't until we hear what she has to say."

"Okay, let's get this over with." Noah quickened his step, propelling her forward with him.

Mrs. Brown rose and offered her hand to both Cara and Noah. "I'm glad you could come on such short notice." She indicated the student desks in front of hers.

Cara nearly laughed watching Noah squeeze into the small chair and quickly averted her gaze, encountering Mrs. Brown's stern one. She fidgeted in her seat as if she was back in the classroom and nine years old.

"I know that Russell has only been with us two weeks and that there's always a period of adjustment, but today was the last straw." The teacher's voice mirrored her expression.

"What did *Rusty* do?" Noah straightened as best he could in the confining desk.

"He tried to extort a classmate's lunch money."

"What happened?"

The steel thread woven through Noah's voice chilled Cara. She folded her arms across her chest.

"When the child wouldn't give him the money, Russell started a fight on the playground. I caught him before any real harm was done."

"Where is he?" His hands curled into fists.

"He's in the principal's office, waiting to go home. He's been suspended the rest of this day and Monday and Tuesday of next week." Mrs. Brown opened a drawer and withdrew a sheet of paper. "Look at this picture he did yesterday. He's an angry young man."

Noah stared at the drawing then passed it to Cara. Bold slashing lines sliced through the family of four standing in front of a house that surprisingly looked like the one the boy had been living in until recently.

"The class was making a picture of the story we'd just finished reading. I'd even commented to him right before he did that about how good the drawing was. When I walked to the next table, Russell did that. I think he needs counseling."

Noah wiggled his way out of the student desk and stood. "He'll get it. I'll see to it."

Cara hurried after Noah, who strode from the classroom. In the hallway he halted, his arms stiff at his sides. She laid a hand on his back, and he wheeled around.

"I thought things were going okay. He's been good since those first few days." He unfurled his fists and rolled his shoulders.

"Maybe too good. With all that's happened to him lately, he should be showing more anger."

"I thought, once Adam got there, he felt his family was complete. He settled down then." Noah plunged his fingers through his hair. "I don't know what to do, Cara. Have you had this kind of problem with Timothy? No, forget I even asked that. Timothy is a good kid."

"Believe me, that wasn't always the case. Right after his dad died, he was mad at me, at the world. He acted out a lot for several months."

"What did you do?"

"Loved him and I had him talk with our minister, who was also a counselor. Slowly Timothy was able to open up to him and not keep everything inside."

"That was important?"

"Yes. If I hadn't had Laura when Tim died, I don't know what I would have done. Everybody at one time or another needs to share their burdens. Otherwise they fester and grow until they do more damage."

A mask fell over his features as if he was retreating into a shell. "So we get him counseling, then what?"

"Love him and let him know that we're here for him." As she spoke, the rightness of the words emphasized how close she had grown to the children in just two weeks. She felt as though she and Noah were a team and that scared her. This whole situation was only temporary. It could end at any time—just as soon as the state found a foster family to take in all three children. Yet the estate felt like home to her and—even worse—to her son.

"I'll talk to Laura and Peter and see who they can recommend. I want the best for Rusty."

Cara stepped back, needing some physical distance from Noah. "In the meantime I want to get them involved at church. They enjoyed going last Sunday. I think Adam will benefit from the youth group and there are some activities for the younger children they should enjoy."

"I don't want them to feel forced into going to church."

"Did you feel like that?"

Any relaxation in his body disappeared. He nodded

once, then spun on his heel and strode toward the principal's office at the end of the corridor.

What had happened to Noah? Again she wondered if this was why she was drawn to him—to help him find his way to the Lord. His wounds ran deep and had never healed—even though she suspected he thought they had. *Father, I need Your help on this one. I feel in over my head.*

Outside the principal's office Noah and Rusty waited for her. She hurried down the hall. Both of them had blank expressions, the high wall around their emotions firmly in place.

Her task wouldn't be easy, but maybe then she would feel she had a purpose. After Tim's death she'd experienced an aimlessness, as if she were wandering around in the desert looking for a home, much like the Hebrews after they fled Egypt. Although the kids helped her feel needed, being with them was only temporary.

Noah escorted her and Rusty to her Chevy. "I have a meeting this afternoon. I'll be home after that," he said in a clipped voice, then walked away.

On the drive to the estate the stony silence and Rusty's rebellious expression reinforced her resolve to make a difference in his life—and Noah's.

When she pulled into the drive, the child asked, "Am I grounded?"

"What do you think we should do?" She and Noah hadn't discussed this, and she realized she wasn't his temporary guardian and really didn't have a say in what happened.

She came to a stop at the side of the house near the garage. Without a word he thrust open the car door and jumped out.

Cara climbed out and watched the child run toward the

back entrance. When she mounted the steps to the deck, Rusty waited for her, his arms folded over his chest, a scowl on his face.

She unlocked the door and entered.

He stormed into the house, his arms now by his sides, anger in every line of his body. "Am I grounded?" he shouted.

Realizing he was desperately seeking boundaries, she pivoted. "Go to your room and we will discuss it when Noah comes home. In the meantime think about why you tried to extort money and got into a fight."

He brushed past her and raced up the stairs two at a time. The slamming of his bedroom door vibrated through the house. The stomping of his footsteps across his room to his bed demonstrated his fury.

Father, please give me the patience to help Rusty and Noah to see Your forgiveness and love.

"Are you at least going to file assault and battery charges against them?" Cara gripped the phone so tight pain shot down her arm.

"Yes, we will be formally charging them on Monday. Our case is stronger for that. Attempted kidnapping would only be your word against the three young men and right now the press is on their side. I'll keep you informed about any developments. I'll have to prep you for your testimony at the trial."

When Cara hung up from talking to the assistant district attorney, she couldn't contain her trembling. It spread through her like a wildfire. Her honesty had never been questioned before, and she wasn't sure what she could do about it.

She sank onto the chair at the desk and buried her face

in her hands. Only this morning before going to meet with Rusty's teacher, she had read an article in the paper about what upstanding young men Jake, Brent and Jeremy were, that they had never been in trouble until now. The piece had come close to wondering if she had lied to get attention.

She scrubbed her hands down her face and sat up straight when she heard the French doors opening. Thankfully all the children but Rusty would be at the farm helping with the animals so she didn't have to see them right now. But she would have to see Noah.

His footsteps crossed the hardwood floor of the great room. She glanced at him as he came into the kitchen nook. A question entered his gaze as it skimmed over her features.

"Has Rusty been giving you trouble?"

She shook her head, words lodged in her throat.

"Then what's wrong?" He sat at the table.

"I just talked with the assistant district attorney. He's moving forward on the charges of assault and battery but dropping the attempted kidnapping ones."

"I'm not surprised."

"But—"

He held up his hand. "Only because he wants to present the strongest case, the one he thinks he has a chance to win. I know they should be charged with both, but neither Adam nor I can testify to the attempted kidnapping."

"I know the truth, even if everyone else doesn't." Anger laced her words.

"And I believe you one hundred percent. Don't ever doubt that."

His reassurances comforted her, and some of her

tension melted. "Thanks. After that article in the paper, I feel a little vulnerable."

Noah frowned. "What article? I haven't read the paper yet."

"I tore it up. But the reporter made it clear that the three ballplayers were being railroaded by me and that I was standing in their way of going pro."

"You certainly aren't in the way of them playing for a pro team. The truth will come out in the end."

"Thanks for saying that, but we both know it doesn't always."

"It will in this case." His jaw hardened.

She prayed he was right. "I'm glad you're home before I have to pick up the other children at the farm. We need to discuss how to handle Rusty and what he did at school. He asked me if he was grounded. He didn't like my answer. I asked him what we should do. He didn't have an answer. Since this is your decision as his guardian—"

"No, it is *our* decision. You're with them more on a daily basis and certainly far more knowledgeable than me on how to handle children."

His declaration appeased some of the self-doubt creeping into her thoughts ever since reading that newspaper article this morning.

"I know Rusty needs boundaries," Cara said. "I don't know that he's had much of that in his life. Children need structure. They need to know what is acceptable and not acceptable. But at the same time I did want to know what he thought we should do with him. I also believe children should reflect on their behavior."

"Okay, let's come up with a game plan, then have a talk with him."

When Noah didn't say anything further, Cara truly

realized how out of his league this parenting gig was. "First, he needs to apologize to the student involved in the incident. And I think as long as he is suspended, he should be grounded. He shouldn't watch TV or go anywhere."

"He doesn't watch much TV and he certainly doesn't go anywhere."

"Then no video games, which I know he likes to play, and he should have some chores to do around here while he's home. Maybe it will make him feel more a part of this place."

"Okay," Noah rose, "that sounds fine by me. Let's get this over with."

Cara came to her feet and headed upstairs to Rusty's bedroom with Noah next to her, a united front, something she had never really felt with Tim. She'd been the only one to discipline Timothy. Her husband wouldn't have anything to do with it.

Noah knocked on Rusty's door, then opened it and entered the room. Curled on his side, the child kept his back to them as he lay on the bed.

"We need to talk about what happened at school." Noah threw an "it's your turn" glance at her.

"Rusty, why did you feel you had to extort money from your classmate?" The stiffening of the boy's back was the only sign he heard what she had said.

Noah started to say something. Cara touched his arm and shook her head. He clamped his mouth close.

Finally when the silence had lengthened to a few minutes, Rusty rolled over and sat up. "I wanted some money. Why else would I have done it?" Defiance marked his expression. "You won't let me get a job."

Cara wanted to be on eye level with the child, so she pulled out the desk chair and sat while Noah positioned himself next to her. "You're only nine. Your job is to go to school and do the best you can."

"I want my own spending money."

"If you need money, come to me." Noah placed his hand on the top of the chair slats.

A pout puckered Rusty's mouth. "I don't wanna have to come to you every time I need a handout."

"It's not a handout."

Rusty glared at Noah. "Yes, it is. I'm a charity case. I can earn my own way in this world."

My, such tough words from the boy. Cara hurt for him and could identify with him. She was trying her best to find her place in the world, too. Although she was glad for the housekeeping job, was the real reason Noah offered it to her that he thought of her as a charity case? It didn't sit well if that were true.

Noah tensed. "Okay, then I'll give you chores around here so you can earn some money. But that won't start until you go back to school. Until then you are grounded from TV, video games and going anywhere."

"Except to church on Sunday," Cara quickly added.

Rusty's glare narrowed even more.

"And you have to apologize to the boy you fought with when you go back to school."

"I ain't apologizing."

"Then you'll remain grounded until you do." Noah met the child's gaze with determination. "It's your choice what happens."

Rusty turned away and faced the wall, his shoulder hunched.

Cara wanted to hug the boy, take all his troubles away—as she did Noah! Oh, my, where had that come from? That realization threatened her heart.

"I'm going to pick up Adam and Lindsay. We'll have dinner after I get back." Cara pushed herself up and crossed to the hallway.

"I ain't hungry," Rusty grumbled.

"Suit yourself." Noah left right behind Cara and pulled the door close. "I'm not sure that went well."

She shrugged. "It's hard to tell. The test will come when he goes back to school."

"I picture him being grounded for weeks. He's pretty stubborn."

"But someone stubborn can get bored and decide to cut his losses. You'll be here?"

"Yeah."

"I'll be at Laura's for a while before bringing the kids home. I wanted to catch up on what's been going on with her."

"I'll keep an eye on Rusty. Take all the time you need. You certainly haven't taken any time off since you started the job. This wasn't supposed to be a 24/7 job."

"Then you don't know anything about being a parent." The second she said the sentence she wanted to snatch it back. She wasn't Rusty's parent, but she felt like it, especially lately.

Noah caught her gaze. "No, that's why I was wise enough to hire you to help. See you when I see you."

Cara hurried downstairs and grabbed her purse. The drive to the farm only took twenty minutes—twenty minutes that she spent trying to talk herself out of not becoming any more involved in Noah or the children's lives. She knew she wouldn't listen to that little warning voice in her head because she already cared.

Besides, how could she turn away from what the Lord wanted her to do?

She parked in front of Laura's house and found her friend in the kitchen, making two more pecan pies while the first ones were baking in the oven. The aroma suffused the air with tempting sweetness.

"Okay, maybe I need to stay for dinner. I love pecan pie." Cara took another deep inhalation.

"They aren't for dinner. Remember the bake sale Sunday at church. These are my contribution. I'm going to be so busy tomorrow, I had to make them today."

"Now I know what I'll be buying at the sale. Lindsay and I are baking chocolate chip cookies tomorrow."

Laura opened the oven door and removed the two pies and put the others in to bake. "How's everything going? I haven't had much time to talk to you lately. There have been several problems with the fourth house."

Cara walked to the coffeepot and poured a mug. "Rusty got in trouble at school today."

Laura fixed herself a cup, too. "I know. The kids told me."

"He's so angry. Do you know a good counselor?"

"Yes, Shane McCoy. He's worked with some of our children. He's the best child psychologist in the area. I'll call him and see if he can work Rusty in. His schedule is usually full because he's in such demand but he owes me a favor."

Cara leaned back against the counter and sipped her coffee. "I appreciate any help you can give us."

Amazement shimmered in Laura's gaze. "Us? That sounds serious."

"I mean Rusty and me, not Noah and me."

"Ah, yes, I'm sure you don't mean Noah and you. He doesn't get serious *ever*."

"You don't have to remind me. I'm perfectly aware of that."

"Good, because I don't want you to get hurt. He doesn't mean to hurt the women he dates. He's always upfront at the beginning about his intentions. But I've seen in the two years I've known him more than one think they can change him and end up being hurt. I don't want that for you. You've had enough grief in your life."

"Amen." Cara lifted her mug in a silent toast, then took a swallow of the warm brew.

"How does Timothy like the estate?"

"Well, let's see. It has a pool, a pond with ducks on it, several acres of land and a game room that any kid could lose himself in for hours. On top of that Timothy and Rusty are forming a friendship. Lindsay tries to follow them around and they try to hide."

"You know if I was grounded there, I wouldn't be too upset."

Cara chuckled. "Come to think of it, you're right. Rusty, though, can't play video games and I plan to put him to work while he's off from school. It won't be a vacation."

"I have a feeling Rusty isn't used to following too many rules."

Cara finished the last of her brew then set the mug in the sink. "The little I've gotten from Adam, their father didn't set too many boundaries for them. Speaking of Adam, I'd better go get him and the other two."

"I'll call the barn and have them meet you by your car. I'm afraid if you show up there you'll never get away. We have a litter of kittens that were left not too long ago that all the kids—and me—have gone crazy over."

Cara started for the back door. "Thanks. You're right. If I saw the kittens, I'd want to keep one or two, and the estate isn't my home. I don't feel I can bring a pet into the place, especially when Noah hasn't had much to do with pets. Molly is about all he can deal with right now."

"Ha! You've noticed. When he's in the barn helping, he's like a fish out of water. But he is getting better."

"Yeah, he's getting good running the other way when Molly spies him or he ends up getting a tongue bath." Cara opened the door. "Thanks for calling Dr. McCoy."

Outside the warm spring air caressed her and teased her with nature's scent, a hint of a sweet flowery aroma. She rounded the house and climbed into her blue Chevy as the kids came from the barn, Timothy and Lindsay racing ahead of Adam, who lumbered down the road with his crutches.

Lindsay shrugged out of her backpack and flung it on the seat while Timothy carefully placed his on the floor in back. Adam maneuvered into the front.

"Did you all get a lot done today?" Cara switched on the engine and started down the gravel road.

"I did. I helped Roman with the new horse." Lindsay grinned from ear to ear. "She let me pat her a lot. I want to learn to ride one."

"How about you guys?" Cara's gaze fell on Adam then on her son before she pulled out onto the highway.

"I couldn't do much but watch," Adam said with a frown. "I'll be glad when I get my walking cast."

"Timothy?" Cara glimpsed her son in the rearview mirror. He averted his head and stared out the side window.

"He didn't do much. He spent all his time with the kittens," Lindsay piped up.

Timothy swung around and glowered at the little girl next to him. "I did, too! Someone needed to love them. They were abandoned."

The word abandoned put an immediate damper on the mood in the car, and the rest of the trip passed in silence. By the time Cara turned onto the street that led to Noah's estate, she'd decided to say something about their father's desertion. But as she neared the estate, words froze in her throat as she took in the scene outside the front gate.

Chapter Eight

"What's going on?" Adam sat up straight in the front passenger's seat and stared out the windshield.

Cara slowed the car to a crawl while trying to decide what to do. Her gaze never left the throng of people carrying signs, gathered on the street by Noah's gate. Some of the placards had vile comments about her splashed across them in bold red-and-black letters. A news van passed her and came to a stop near the protestors.

This was the time she wished there was a back way into Noah's estate. She even considered parking down the road and having the kids climb over the eight-foot fence, but then one glance at Adam's crutches nixed that plan. There was only one thing she could do—go forward and get through the handful of protestors as quickly as she could.

She gripped the steering wheel and sent up a silent prayer to the Lord. *I need You. Help me get the children inside without an incident.*

As she continued forward increasing her speed to

fifteen miles per hour, Adam looked over at her. His expression of support gave her the courage to proceed. She plastered on her face what she hoped was a brave front for the children, although inside she trembled and wasn't sure the glue that held her together would stick for long.

As a television reporter began interviewing people, everyone's attention shifted to the TV crew. Cara took the opportunity to advance toward the gate and push the button to open it.

Although the iron railing of the entry made little sound, the noise proclaimed her approach as if she had shouted it over a loudspeaker. Every man and woman spun toward the car, lifting his or her posters and yelling at her.

"Everything will be all right once we get inside. Don't worry. I'll explain then." Cara schooled her voice to the calmest level she could manage while her stomach became rock hard and constricted.

Could this day get any worse?

A couple of big men with no signs rushed the car and banged on the hood as she passed them. The sound resonated through the interior, causing Lindsay to scream.

Cara glanced back at the little girl, offering a half smile. Tears flooded her eyes and ran down her thin cheeks. "We'll be okay. They won't do anything with the news crew filming what's happening." She hoped. She prayed.

Ten feet and they would be safely inside the gate.

Shouts of rage surrounded them as Cara pressed her foot on the brake to decrease her speed to a few miles per hour.

Five feet.

Someone struck the trunk. Cara flinched and spied a young college-aged woman glaring at her. She hit the back of the car again and gave Cara an obscene gesture.

Mercifully the gate closed behind the car, and Cara picked up speed, racing toward the back, away from the prying eyes of the crowd peering at them through the iron bars. When she parked behind the mansion near the garage, she wanted to collapse against the steering wheel, but she was aware of the children's confused gazes on her.

Taking several deep breaths, she calmed her hammering heartbeat. "Charges were filed against the three men who bothered me in The Ultimate Pizzeria parking lot a few weeks ago. Those people weren't happy about it."

Timothy, with saucer-round eyes, twisted so he could look toward the driveway that led to the gate. "Why are they mad at you? Those men did wrong."

"Honey, they think I'm lying about what happened."

He came back around and sat forward. "You don't lie."

"You and I know that, but some don't."

"Well, I can tell them." Timothy put his hand on the handle.

"No!"

Her son froze.

"You didn't lie, and I can tell them that," Adam declared.

His fervent tone bolstered her spirits. Cara looked from the teen to the children in back. "I want you all to promise me you won't have anything to do with those people out there. Don't go near the gate or fence. Promise."

Adam gave a curt nod.

"I won't, Mom."

"Me, too," Lindsay said between sobs.

"Let's get inside. I've got a dinner to fix."

The whole way to the house, Cara scanned the area, half expecting someone with a sign to pop up from behind a bush and try to stop her. Relief didn't descend even when she finally closed the French doors, because the second she faced Noah she knew he didn't realize what was going on outside his gate. His puzzled expression quickly grew into one of deep concern as his attention flickered from Adam to Timothy to Lindsay, still crying, and then came to rest on Cara.

"What happened?" he asked.

"You all go on and start your homework upstairs in your rooms." Cara wouldn't look at Noah.

"But it's Fri—" Adam's protest faded as he stared at Cara. "Come on, Lindsay and Timothy. I'll let you ride the elevator to the second floor with me."

When the room cleared of children, Noah walked to her and stood in front so she had to look at him. "Okay, tell me what's going on."

She wanted to make light of the situation, but she still quivered from the animosity she felt as she drove through the demonstrators. She needed to sit and barely made it to the nearest chair before she collapsed into it, squeezing her hands together.

"Cara, you've got me worried."

Tears pooled in her eyes as she peered up at him, hovering in front of her. "There are some people who aren't too happy with me for filing charges against Jake, Brent and Jeremy."

"We knew that would happen. Why are you so upset right now?"

"Because there's a group of them camped out in front of your gate with posters announcing to the world exactly what they think of me. And let me tell you, they don't think I'm the girl next door."

Fury hardened his features into a fierce expression. He pivoted and headed for the front door.

Cara leaped to her feet and raced after him, stopping him before he left the house. "No, I don't want you to get hurt. There are at least ten of them."

"I don't care. They can't protest on private property."

"I think they're usually in the street by the curb."

"Usually?"

"When I pulled up and the gate opened, they surrounded the car. Thankfully a news crew was there filming or I'm not sure what would have happened." A shiver slithered down her spine, and cold burrowed deep into her bones.

He glanced back at the door.

"Please, Noah. I don't want to give the press any more than they already have."

"They aren't going to stay out front." He marched into his study and grabbed the phone, punching in a series of numbers.

The lethal quiet in his voice as he spoke to the chief of police made Cara glad he was on her side. He appeared calm and in control except for a tic twitching in his jaw. With his protective facade firmly in place, he hung up and rotated toward her.

"The police will be here soon to clear them away."

"That will only make things worse."

"They trespassed on my property when they surrounded your car at the gate. I will file charges against each one if they don't leave. I'm sure it was caught on tape by the TV crew. If not, it was on my security camera at the gate."

"Still—"

He quickly covered the distance between them and pressed his finger to her lips. "Don't you worry about a thing. You are safe here. I won't let anything happen to you or the children."

His touch traced the outline of her mouth. Her eyes slid closed at the wonderful feel of his rough skin grazing hers. She wanted to melt against him, surrender to the safety she knew would be in his embrace.

But Laura's earlier words assailed her. He wasn't the marrying kind and that was all she could ever be.

She pulled back. "I need to get dinner started or we'll have a rebellious crew on our hands."

"I'm going to watch the monitor and make sure they leave. I'll be in the study if you need me."

As she prepared spaghetti and meat sauce, she tuned into the news. While cutting up an onion, she stopped mid-slice when the footage shot in front of the gate came on.

A picture of her blue Chevy with ten or so people encircling it showed in the background while the reporter said, "As you can see there are some angry protestors outside the home of Noah Maxwell, the owner of The Ultimate Pizzeria Southwest chain of restaurants. Inside the car is Cara Winters, the woman behind the charges being brought against three star baseball players for the Cimarron City University's team. Jake Ramsey, Brent Bright and Jeremy Newcastle are facing possible jail time if they are convicted of assault and battery. The team's hopes of a conference championship are jeopardized by this new development—"

Her hand trembling, Cara flipped the station and the inane music of a game show played while contestants vied for a prize. The reporter had made it sound as though Cara was the reason the players would go to jail—not their actions.

A strong urge to flee the town flowed through her. She had done nothing wrong, yet she was paying dearly for reporting the young college students' terrifying behavior.

Her legs weak, she leaned into the kitchen counter to keep herself upright. She was a fighter. With the Lord's help, she would come out of this stronger.

On Saturday a week later Cara sat at the kitchen table, finishing her cup of coffee while Noah downed the rest of his. "Are you sure you want to do this? All three can be a handful."

"Who should I tell to stay back?"

"Maybe I should come with you."

"I'm not totally hopeless when it comes to the children. They have been here three weeks, and I think I've done pretty good if you forget about the kitten incident."

"I can but I'm not sure they can." Cara fought to keep her laughter inside but it leaked through.

"Okay, I didn't realize Timothy had sneaked a kitten from the farm. I thought I was rescuing a stray by taking him to Peter."

"I think they sneaked it in that day they had their backpacks and I picked them up after school at Laura's. I didn't have a clue there was a kitten in the pool cabana."

"A kitten that definitely was tired of being confined in there, judging by the pitiful whines," Noah said wryly.

"Have you decided about going back to get the kitten or not?"

A frown furrowed Noah's forehead. "What about Molly? She's so big and the kitten is so small."

"That puppy doesn't have a mean bone in her body. I think it will be fine." Cara saw her son peep around the corner into the kitchen. "Timothy wanted me to ask you if he could keep the kitten. He says you won't even know it's here."

"Why don't you ask me yourself, Timothy?" Noah twisted around in his chair and looked straight at her son.

With his head down, Timothy shuffled into the room. "Can I keep Bosco?"

"Yes, but you need to make sure Molly and Bosco get along okay. Can you be responsible for that?"

Timothy nodded, a huge grin on his face.

"Then we'll go over to the farm after we go fishing and pick Bosco up."

Her son pumped his arm in the air, saying, "Yes!" then ran from the kitchen shouting for Rusty.

"I didn't have the heart to tell him I think I'm allergic to cats. I sneezed the whole way to the farm with Bosco in my car." Noah rose and took his mug to the sink.

"You are? Then maybe this isn't a good idea. I can get him a pet when we've permanently settled somewhere."

Noah's eyebrows slashed downward. "No, Timothy has definitely bonded with Bosco."

Cara tried to read the strange look that passed over Noah's face, but she couldn't tell exactly what he was feeling, which wasn't that much of a surprise. He was very good at concealing his emotions, she suspected from years of experience. "Then I'll make sure he keeps the kitten away from you."

"And Molly."

"For never having had a pet, you're certainly getting into this. I saw you tossing Molly a ball out back yesterday."

He dismissed her comment with a wave of his hand. "She needs exercise."

"Yeah, right."

He pinched his mouth into a mock frown. "She does! I'll get the fishing equipment from the cabana and meet y'all by the pool."

He hurried from the kitchen before he revealed the turmoil racing through him. Why had Cara's comment about finding a permanent place bothered him? This was temporary. From the beginning that had been clear to both of them. And yet, picturing her someplace other than his guesthouse didn't seem right.

He glanced back at his place and for the first time really saw it as a home. Before it had been just a house for him to come home to, unwind and sleep. Now something was different, and if he thought long enough on it, he was sure it was because of Cara and the children.

Panic bubbled to the surface. It was just the novelty of the situation. Soon it would wear off and he would be yearning for his carefree, no-strings-attached kind of life. There was just so much bickering, whining, pouting, laughing and hugging a guy could take. Most of his experience with families wasn't good. He had to remember that. Those couple of years with the Hendersons were the exception.

Out in the cabana he quickly gathered up the fishing poles and his tackle box. By the time he emerged the children and Cara were waiting by the pool watching Molly swim.

He tried to skirt her as she came out of the pool, but she homed in on him, flapping her head and spraying him with water. Then, as usual, the puppy jumped up, resting her paws on his chest as she licked him in greeting.

In his toughest voice, Noah said, "Down, Molly. Down."

A few more slobbers of her tongue and she obeyed.

"She likes you," Cara said, laughter in her voice.

"I kinda get that, but why?"

"Because she sees a pet lover in the making."

Noah pointed to himself. "Me? No way."

Without a word, Rusty took the pole Noah handed him. Although the boy had apologized to the child he'd had problems with at school, he had made it clear by his silence he hadn't wanted to. Other than when he had to, he didn't talk to Cara or him. At least Noah heard him converse with the other kids.

The children ran ahead while Noah walked with Cara at a more sedate pace. "I'm glad they're getting better with their swimming lessons."

"Lindsay actually paddled all the way across the pool yesterday. Rusty is a natural, like Timothy. I wish Adam could have come along, but I'm glad he's pitching in at the farm."

"Peter told me he's following Roman around and asking all kinds of questions about the animals. He told me this summer he wanted to work at a vet's."

"What did you say?"

"I told him if he was still with me I thought that was a good idea." He didn't tell Cara about the disappointment he'd seen in Adam's eyes because he couldn't explain the disappointment he'd felt when talking with the teen.

"The assistant D.A. called yesterday."

Noah slowed his pace even more and took in Cara's tense features. "And?"

"The trial will start the week after next on Thursday."

"I'm thinking the college wants this settled before the championship series, if they make it. The team is having problems with the three players benched, pending the verdict of your case and the public intoxication charges. Too bad the D.A. dropped the DUI against Brent since they were parked when the police appended them," Noah said.

"There are more than a few people not happy with me because they're not playing. I didn't get to tell you what happened at the grocery store yesterday."

Halting, Noah faced Cara, knowing he wasn't going to like what she had to say.

"A man chewed me out at the checkout counter. Then another said something I won't repeat as I left. In my haste I forgot to get your sales receipt. I thought about going back to get it, but I'd rather pay for the groceries myself than—"

"Shh." Anger gripped him. "You won't pay for anything. I don't need a receipt. I admire your honesty and know you would never try to rip me off."

She lifted glistening eyes to him. "Are you sure?"

"Oh, yeah, I'm very sure. In fact, I don't need a receipt from now on. I never did. I trust you."

"But I'd rather—"

He moved in closer, stopping the flow of her words. "No, I'm the employer. You have to do what I say."

She looked into his eyes for a long moment, then burst out laughing until tears ran down her cheeks. "Don't let this boss thing go to your head."

He loved the sound of her laughter. It wormed its way into his heart, making him vulnerable to her. How had he ever seen her as a plain woman? There was nothing ordinary and unattractive about her.

"Mom! C'mon!"

"Our troops await us or rather you since you won't ever get me to bait a hook or take a fish off the line." Cara started toward her son, who stood by the pond with his feet braced apart and holding his pole like a spear.

The warm April sun glittered across the water's mirror-like surface. A male mallard duck took flight, his mate following. Another one paddled across the pond with her brood trailing after her.

"See the babies, Cara?" Lindsay pointed at the family, the male duck taking up the rear. "I didn't see them the last time I came down here."

"I found a nest under that bush." Timothy nodded his head toward a large shrub halfway on the other side. "I wonder if those are the babies."

"Can we go check?" Lindsay tugged on Timothy's arm.

"Not now. I want to fish." Cara's son shrugged away from the little girl.

"I'll take you." Cara offered Lindsay her hand. "We'll let the guys fish while we explore."

Noah watched Cara and Lindsay begin to circle the pond until Rusty started rummaging through his bait box.

"Where are the worms?" the nine-year-old asked, a challenging look on his face.

"I don't fish with worms. Too messy. I use hot dogs."

"Hot dogs? I've never heard of that. Everyone uses worms."

"My fish haven't heard that one. I've never had any trouble catching some when I use my special bait."

Humphing, Rusty rose. Skepticism wrinkled his forehead as he squinted at Noah. The boy glanced toward Timothy as though his friend would come to his defense.

"Tell you what. I'll use my hot dog bait while you dig for a worm and use that. Let's see who get a fish first."

Rusty's face brightened. "I will." He scanned the area, decided on a place to dig and began searching for a worm.

"Timothy, which do you want to use?" Noah asked, getting a hot dog out to cut into small pieces.

Cara's son peered at his friend then at him. Finally

Timothy gestured toward Rusty. Friendship had won out, as it should. Noah smiled as he observed them burrowing a hole into the earth, a small hill of dirt building up between the boys.

Laughter drifted to Noah. In the distance by the bush Lindsay peered through the foliage. Even from where he was, he could tell she was excited. Then suddenly a snow goose charged out from under the scrub and darted for her. Cara stepped in between the girl and the enraged goose. It nipped Cara on the bare part of her leg.

Lindsay whirled about and ran back toward Noah. Cara came at a slower pace, limping slightly. The goose pursued her part of the way, honking. Both of the boys, the knees of their jeans encrusted with mud, stood and stared at the animal flapping its wings.

Rusty held a wiggling worm between his forefinger and thumb. "I've got my bait."

Empty-handed, Timothy trudged after his friend. "I guess I'd better use the hot dog."

A few minutes later as Cara and Lindsay approached, the boys attempted to cast their lines out into the water. Rusty succeeded; Timothy snarled his.

Noah quickly put a hot dog on his hook, launched it out into the middle of the pond, then gave the pole to Lindsay. "If you feel a tug, reel it in this way."

After demonstrating to the girl how to bring the fish in, Noah took Timothy's pole and began to untangle it. The line was knotted so badly Noah decided to put it aside. He'd have to fix it later. Until then, he gave Cara's son the last fishing rod and went through the steps with him again.

This time Timothy managed to cast it out a few feet, but Noah could see the tangles in the line. He groaned.

The boy sent him a sorrowful frown. "I'm sorry. I didn't mean to mess it up."

"That's okay. Leave it in. It's no big deal."

The child's eyes grew saucer round. "It isn't?"

"Nope."

When Timothy moved down next to Rusty, Cara came to Noah's side and leaned close. His heartbeat picked up speed while her scent of vanilla dominated all others.

"Thanks," she whispered.

"For what?"

"For not making a big deal out of the snarled lines. Timothy can get extra sensitive about messing up."

"Why? Isn't that part of learning?" He might not have parenting down, but it was a no-brainer that children would make mistakes while learning new things. He certainly had and still did.

"Yes, but my husband didn't tolerate mistakes well to the point that Timothy rarely tried something new."

"I've got something!" Lindsay jumped up and down, losing her hold on the rod.

Noah lunged toward the pole as it flew out of the girl's hand. He landed with a splash in the pond. Bringing his head up, he saw his best fishing rod for the last time when it disappeared under the water in the middle. He contemplated, since he was already wet, swimming out to where it had vanished and diving down to search for the pole.

Lindsay's sobs halted that thought. She danced about on the shore, gesturing toward the water. "I didn't mean to let it go. I'm sorry. I'm sorry."

Noah pushed himself to his feet, his tennis shoes drenched, along with the rest of him. The humor in the situation struck him, and he began to laugh. "I seem to be constantly in a soaked state. I promise you guys I take a shower every day."

The two boys took one look at him and began to giggle while Lindsay quieted. A smile grew on her face as she stared at him.

Noah glanced at Cara, who was trying desperately to hide her laughter behind her hand. "Do I look that bad?"

She walked to him and pulled a plant from his hair, then rubbed her hand along his cheek. "I'm thinking you might need that shower now."

When he saw the mud on her fingertips, he peered down at his tan jeans and light blue T-shirt. Not only were they wet but dark with dirt ground into them, and somehow he'd managed to stir up muck that now covered his white—strike that, brown—tennis shoes.

"Oh, I've got something!" Timothy yelled.

"Hold on to it." Noah hurried to the boy's side.

Cara's son gripped it and looked up at Noah for help. "What do I do now?"

"Reel it in like I showed you." Noah stood behind Timothy, his hand on the boy's shoulder. "You're doing great."

Timothy struggled to bring the fish in. When the medium-sized crappie broke the surface, the boy beamed. "It's a big one!" He swung his pole until he flopped the fish onto the grass along the shore. "Can I have it for dinner, Mom?"

"Sure. We can fry up any edible ones we catch."

"Now you can learn how to take it off the hook, and then you can put it in the bucket next to the bait box."

Rusty tried to ignore them, but when Noah squatted beside Timothy, Rusty sidled over to where Noah was showing Cara's son how to handle the crappie. While

Rusty acted as if he wasn't interested in what they were doing, he kept peeking at them, stepping even closer.

As Timothy baited his hook again, Rusty's lined bobbed. "I've got a hit! I've got a hit!"

"Great! You'll get to eat your own fish." Timothy moved closer to his friend.

Rusty began reeling his catch in, such a big grin on his face that Noah responded with one of his own. He glanced around him, everyone's attention directed at Rusty. Was this what family was about? Cheering each other on? Caring about the other? Remembering his too-brief years with the Hendersons, Noah had to say yes to all three questions. For a short time he had experienced that.

Then why have I turned my back on having a family?

Because for most of his life, he lived in fear, just wanting to survive one day to the next. And then when Whitney came along he had to protect her, and when he didn't, the guilt ate into him. He'd let her down on numerous occasions, and he didn't want to experience that ever again.

Cara finished her preparations for frying the fish the boys caught that day. Along with coleslaw, baked beans and corn bread, there should be enough for dinner tonight. She wouldn't do the crappie until the children and Noah got back from the farm. Although he was allergic to cats, Noah insisted on being the one to pick up the kitten, since he'd taken Bosco there in the first place.

Cara returned the milk to the refrigerator and started back toward the sink when she spied the front of The Ultimate Pizzeria on the news. She quickly adjusted the volume to the TV on the kitchen counter, so she could hear what the reporter was saying.

The same woman who had been in front of the mansion said, "The protests continue concerning the charges being brought against the three star baseball players for the UCC's team. Noah Maxwell, the owner of this restaurant, is one of the witnesses and Cara Winters's employer. This is the site where the alleged incident happened. I have with me one of the leaders of this protest."

As the reporter thrust a microphone into the face of a large, beefy man who Cara recognized as one of the people who had been outside the gate, she flipped the sound down. When was she going to learn? She couldn't listen to the news while fixing dinner, as was her habit. She would need to change her routine in order to keep her composure. She didn't want the children to see what this trial was doing to her.

But she couldn't take her gaze off the television image of people marching with those awful posters in front of Noah's restaurant. She noticed in the background the cars slowing down and the occupants gawking. What a spectacle!

With hands quivering, she reached for the button and turned the set off. The calmness she sought evaded her. Her stomach knotted. Noah didn't deserve this. All he'd tried to do was help her and his business might suffer because of that.

What do I do, Lord?

Thoughts swirled around in her mind, making no sense. Leave. No, fight. Go back to Laura's. Stay and make those men pay for what they did.

What do You want?

The question hung in the air for a long moment. The sound of the French doors opening and children's voices reverberating through the great room in excitement gave her no time to come up with a plan. But she had to talk to Noah. That much she knew.

"Mom! Mom!"

Timothy skidded to a stop just inside the kitchen. He held Bosco up. "He missed me. Hear his purring."

Not giving her son a chance to thrust the kitten at her, she scooped him up into her embrace and hugged him tightly to her. "I love you."

"Mom, you're squashing Bosco."

She pulled back, fighting tears near the surface. "Oh, sorry. I just missed you."

"I was only gone a little while."

A lot changed in an hour, she thought, but kept quiet. Later she would get Noah alone to talk. She wouldn't be responsible for hurting his business or him. As they had become friends, his guard occasionally slipped, and she sensed his vulnerability more and more.

Noah and the other children appeared in the entrance to the kitchen. "We're starved. We had to help out at the barn so I've worked up quite an appetite for those crappie."

"Sure. Lindsay, you and Timothy set the table. Rusty and Adam will do the dishes tonight afterward."

Amid some groans, Cara began frying the fish. "Don't forget to wash your hands."

More groans, then the shuffling of feet as the children all went into the laundry room off the kitchen to use the sink in there. The sounds they made drowned out Cara's thoughts. To get through the dinner she needed to concentrate on something other than the protestors and the upcoming trial, the fact that Tim had always kept her in the dark about what was going on with him. Although Noah and she weren't married, they were friends and employer-employee. She deserved to know everything, even the bad. The time to deal with that would be later when she confronted Noah and asked him why he hadn't told her what was happening at his restaurant.

Chapter Nine

"Are you sure it's all right to have Timothy spend the night with Rusty?" Cara stopped at the top of the staircase after putting Lindsay to sleep.

Noah started down the steps. "Rusty's talking again. I don't want to jeopardize that. As I left them, they were hashing over today's fishing. They're still arguing over who got the biggest crappie."

"They just won't accept it was a tie." Cara followed Noah into the great room, still needing to have that talk with him now that the younger children were in bed. She glanced toward the game room where Adam watched a movie DVD, the sounds of the television drifting to her. "We need to talk. How about out on the deck?"

Noah arched an eyebrow. "This must be serious."

She didn't respond, but instead headed toward the French doors and exited. The cool spring air, heavy with the smell of rain, wrapped around her. At the railing she faced Noah; the light from the floor-to-ceiling windows silhouetted him, casting his features in dimness. Maybe this wasn't such a good idea. Then she remembered how adept he was at masking his true emotions behind a neutral facade. It wouldn't make any difference if she saw his expression or not.

"I saw the six o'clock news tonight and guess what was on it?"

"Another report about the trial?"

"Yes. This one showed your restaurant being picketed where the incident, according to the reporter, *allegedly* happened. Why didn't you tell me?"

He stiffened. "Because it isn't your concern."

He might as well have slammed a door in her face. She stepped away, the railing pressing into her back. "Not my concern? How can you say that?"

"Easy. You aren't working at the restaurant anymore."

"But I'm the reason those people are marching out in front of The Ultimate Pizzeria. Is it hurting business?"

Silence greeted her question.

"Don't bother answering. It is."

"It's been slow since they appeared a few days ago," Noah said.

"Oh, Noah, I'm so sorry."

"Sorry about what?" His voice firmed with anger. "You aren't at fault. Those three guys are. If they think this will make me back down from testifying to the truth, then they don't know me. I won't be blackmailed!"

His declaration should have soothed her, but her stomach twisted into a tighter knot, the anxiety spreading upward to constrict her chest.

He inched closer. She tried to maneuver away but his arms caged her against the railing. "They need to be held accountable for their actions. Being the star players of the baseball team does not make them invincible."

"But what if people stop coming to eat at The Ultimate Pizzeria? I can't have that on my conscience."

"First, I only have four here in Cimarron City. I have ten times that in other places all over Oklahoma, Kansas, Arkansas and Texas." He leaned in, his mouth a breath away.

"You do?" she squeaked, her throat dry, her heart thudding against her chest.

"I've worked for the past twelve years, seventy-hour weeks to build this chain up and I have succeeded. This protest won't bring it down. I won't let that happen. I finally am at a place in my life where I can relax and actually take some time for myself because I've got a good organization in place. Those three punks won't take that away from me."

"You can't control everything." She desperately tried to ignore the scent of coffee and peppermint that bathed her lips with each sentence he uttered.

He cradled her face between his large palms. "We are not in the wrong." He said each word slowly as though giving her time to let its meaning sink in.

The tension melted as he cut any space between them and wound his arms around her. His mouth settled over hers, a gentle caress that quickly evolved into a demanding kiss that whisked away all her stress. The only thing her mind could focus on was the effect Noah had on her. His distinctive scent, the comfort from his embrace, the sense of safety when she was near him.

When he broke away, his ragged breathing attested to the effect she had on him. She'd never felt so feminine as in that moment. She didn't need to see his face to realize that their relationship had changed. Later, she'd probably panic, but right now, a glow encompassed her with a feeling of warmth.

"I shouldn't have done that," he muttered, pivoting away.

Something died in her with those words.

Then he swung back toward her. "But I'm not sorry for kissing you. I've wanted to since I met you."

The sun came out and shone bright in the middle of the night. "You mean when you nearly ran me down or when you drenched me with water?"

He chuckled, raking his hand through his hair. "You aren't gonna let me live that down, are you?"

"Nope. I have to have something to hold over you."

"At least it's not the kitten incident."

"I'm surprised Timothy agreed to spend the night since Bosco has to stay at the cottage."

"It's good to see Rusty and Timothy becoming friends."

Cara lounged against the railing, crossing her arms over her chest. "After his father died, Timothy wouldn't have much to do with his friends in St. Louis. He shut down."

"I thought he had counseling? Didn't that help?"

Only a father's unconditional love will help. "Yes, some, but when Tim died, my son lost his chance to prove himself to his dad. That had become important to Timothy as he grew older."

"Sometimes there's nothing you can do to change the situation. It has taken me years to realize that."

"And you do now?"

Moving farther away, deeper into the dark shadows, he didn't say anything for a long moment. "In my head, yes. I'm still working on my heart."

He'd begun erecting the wall he kept between himself and others. Her heart cracked. She wished she had back the man who had given her a glimpse inside him. Before he totally retreated, she had to ask him a favor. "The kids wanted me to persuade you to come watch them tomorrow in a play between the two services. Each class puts on a story from the Bible."

"Why didn't they ask me themselves?"

"They know you don't usually go to church, but they were hoping I would convince you to come."

Noah sucked in a deep breath. "Do Adam, Rusty and Lindsay like going with you every week?"

"Lindsay loves it. Adam knew some of the kids in the youth group and the high school Sunday school class, so he's enjoyed getting to know them in a different environment. Rusty is taking longer. Truthfully I'm not sure what he thinks. He reminds me of…" She halted when she realized what she was about to say. Her own guard was down, and for a while there had been no taboo subjects for conversation.

"Of me? Is that what you were gonna say? Rusty and I are a lot alike. I can't deny that."

She gritted her teeth and squeezed her hands into fists. "No child should feel they have to go through life alone."

Even from the shadows Noah transmitted his tension, his stance rigid, defensive. "You think Rusty does?"

"Not yet. Not completely. But he's getting there."

"And who should he rely on, if not himself?"

"The Lord. No one is alone with the Lord in his life, even when life throws you a curve."

"Do you really believe that?"

Scorn edged his words and blasted her across the space separating them. "With all my heart. He's been with me when I contemplated divorcing Tim, when my husband got sick and required my care, when Tim died and left me with a mountain of medical bills to pay, when I held my little boy who cried himself to sleep because his daddy was gone."

"He wasn't with me when my father was beating me."

"Was your heart open to the Lord? Did you believe in Him?"

"When my father was sober he expounded on how much he believed in Christ, then he would start drinking and nothing mattered but the bottle. I figured if he was a believer, then the Lord wasn't real. As far as I could see, his god was alcohol."

His confession, wrenched from the soul, pierced through her defenses. This was the moment she'd been praying for—the moment she could share the most important thing in her life. "Liquor alters a person's perceptions. Maybe your dad did believe, but when he was drinking, he wasn't following what Jesus preached. He became a different man. Don't judge the Word on your father's behavior. Judge it for yourself. Bad things happen to everyone. It's how we deal with them that is important. That's where the Lord comes in. He's our comfort and haven in those bad times. We all need a place to seek peace when the world around us is chaotic."

"I wish it were that simple." Noah scrubbed his hands down his face, turning away from her, staring into the great room as though the light held answers for him.

"It's as simple as letting Him into your heart."

His humorless laugh peppered the air. "I haven't been able to let anyone into my heart. I don't think I'm capable of doing that."

The admission shocked Cara, not because of what he said but because he had admitted it to her. She approached him and laid her hand on his back. "You're capable of doing anything you set your mind to. You survived an awful childhood and became an upstanding citizen who cares about the community and the people in it. You never gave up on yourself."

"But I did on others."

"Did you really? I know how much you care about Alice, Jacob and Peter."

"But they still don't know everything. I always hold a part of my…" He whirled around and gripped her arms. "What are you doing to me? I'm no good for you. I'm no good for anyone. Stay away from me." He jerked away and stormed toward the French doors.

The sound of a door slamming underscored the torment that haunted Noah each day of his life. For a brief moment she had seen his barriers fall away. Not long, but long enough to give her hope she could reach him and help him.

Cara descended the steps to the pool level and circled it. Her footsteps sounded on the stone path in the stillness of the night. The darkness beyond the light strangely comforted her as though, for a while, the world beyond, didn't exist. Her problems with the trial were gone for the time being, giving her a chance to focus on what was happening between her and Noah.

She touched her mouth where he had kissed her earlier. It meant so much to her. She doubted he felt the same. She could count on one hand how many times she'd been kissed as a male would a female while he probably had lost track a long time ago. The realization they looked at the kiss from opposing views devastated her. She was falling in love with a man who didn't fall in love—ever.

"What is all this?" Cara swept her arm across her body, indicating the table set for two in the gazebo.

"Our surprise. What do you think, Mom?"

A white linen cloth covered a table laden with china, crystal and silver. A picnic basket sat on one of the wrought iron chairs. "Did you and Lindsay do all this?"

"Laura helped us. She told us about what her kids had done for her and Peter." Lindsay clutched her teddy bear to her chest, caution in her eyes. "Timothy thought we should do something like that with you and Noah."

Why? she wanted to ask so badly but would do nothing to upset Lindsay, who displayed all her insecurities in the situation. Instead she said, "This is sweet, but I think Noah is working late tonight. He usually does on Wednesday."

Timothy shook his head. "Adam and Rusty made him promise to be home tonight to help with Rusty's project at school."

"Well, then he'll be busy. He won't have time—"

"Mom, you've got to eat and so does Noah. There will be time later. Besides, Adam has been working with Rusty this afternoon so he won't need much help. They think they've got it figured out."

Trapped, unless somehow Noah didn't show up, Cara walked to the basket and opened it. "Who made the food?"

"Laura. At first we were gonna, but I can't cook much so she volunteered." Timothy came to Cara's side with Lindsay right behind him, her face more relaxed. "We have everything taken care of. We've been planning this since Sunday."

"Sunday?"

"Yeah, Noah came to church with us because you asked him. We think he likes you," Timothy announced.

She knelt in front of the two children. "Noah and I are friends like you guys are. That's all, honey."

"But if you marry, I can have a dad."

"And we can have a family. We could live here and not bother anyone. You would hardly know we were here." Lindsay scrunched her stuffed animal against her cheek.

A lump jammed Cara's throat. She swallowed several times before saying, "Noah is working hard to make sure you, Rusty and Adam stay together as a family should be."

Lindsay threw her arms around Cara's neck. "But I want you as my mommy."

Tears misted Cara's eyes as she hugged the child to her. She wanted that, too, but didn't see any possibility of that happening. In a month or two she wouldn't have a job that could support a large family. She wouldn't have a place to live. Her life was in a shambles. What did she have to offer three children, even if the state let her be a foster parent?

Timothy tapped on Cara's shoulder. "Hey, I see Rusty and Adam with Noah. They're coming this way."

Lindsay pulled away, tears coursing down her cheeks. Cara wiped them away as the males paused a few yards from the gazebo.

Noah's puzzlement mirrored her own when she had first seen what the children had done. Adam said something to him. Noah glanced back at the house, then at the gazebo, the look in his eyes one of prey cornered and trying to decide the best way to escape.

Rusty didn't give him a chance to flee. He took Noah's hand and dragged him forward.

Oh, great! After their conversation Saturday night, she and Noah had been avoiding spending any time alone. His last words that evening still echoed through her mind at the oddest moments. *I'm no good for you. I'm no good for anyone. Stay away from me.*

Laura's warning against thinking Noah would ever make a commitment, coupled with what he'd said, cautioned her to protect herself as best she could. The sad truth was it was too late. She couldn't stay away from him. She loved him. There was nothing she could do about it other than be here for him for as long as he needed her.

Positioned on the other side of the small table, Noah stared at the finery laid out before him. "This isn't my china and crystal. I don't have any. Whose is it?" He turned toward the kids.

With his walking cast, Adam was hobbling away. Rusty, Timothy and Lindsay, closer to the adults, glanced at each other, wheeled around and raced toward the house, passing the teen.

Noah peered back at Cara, both eyebrows rising. "Should I be concerned?"

She laughed and noticed the slight quaver running through it. "It depends. All this is Laura's, so they didn't come by any of it illegally. But the intent was matchmaking, which probably should concern you." *Especially since you don't want a relationship.*

"Laura's! She went in on this with the kids?"

"Yep." She might as well tell him everything. "They thought if we got married, they could stay here and their family would be together."

Noah opened his mouth for a few seconds, then snapped it close, his eyes wide as he took in the romantic setting. Although it was still light out, candles in hurricane glasses were lit and one of the children had switched on soft classical music, strains of Brahms floating on the air.

"I know. It leaves you speechless." Cara put the lid on the basket and started to lift it off the chair. "I hate for all this good food to go to waste. We can eat it back at the house with the children while we let them know this—"

"Stay, Cara. This is kind of sweet that they cared enough to go to all this trouble."

The awe in his voice stunned her. She'd thought he would run away as fast as the kids had a few moments ago. "If you're sure. This could send the wrong signal to them."

He came around and pulled a chair out for her. After she took a seat, he pushed it toward the table, then leaned down and whispered into her ear, "We can straighten them out later."

She shivered as his warm breath caressed the side of her neck. Unable to say a word, she nodded.

He settled into the chair across from her. "I love Laura's cooking, but I'm gonna miss yours tonight."

His gaze fastened onto hers and kept her spellbound for a few seconds. Finally she slid her look away and took off the basket lid again, studying its contents while she could feel him continuing to study her.

"I like how you're wearing your hair. Did you get it cut today?"

He noticed! Heat singed her cheeks. "Yes. I went to Laura's hairdresser. Summer's coming and I wanted it cut short." She laid the containers of food on the table. "The way Timothy's taken to the water I know he'll want to go swimming a lot."

"They all have enjoyed it. Even Lindsay is becoming quite the little swimmer."

They were discussing a safe subject. Cara relaxed in her chair while Noah removed the tops on each container. "Once she got over the initial fear she had about swimming, she took to it like a natural. I'm not sure she would have learned if we hadn't persuaded her to."

"Fear can cause people to do things they normally wouldn't do. Fear was what prompted me to make my position to Lindsay clear. I would have drained the pool if she hadn't learned. I was afraid she might fall in when no one was around and drown."

"The boys whining probably had a lot to do with it, too."

He chuckled. "They can be mighty persuasive."

"Sometimes I think they have too much energy." Cara forked a slice of ham smothered in a pineapple glaze onto her plate, then dished up some potato salad as well as a seven-layer one.

When Noah had finished serving himself, Cara bowed her head and waited for him to do likewise. "Father, bless this dinner that our friend fixed and the children who so lovingly put it together. We are blessed to have them in our lives. Amen."

"Amen," Noah whispered.

Cara hadn't even been sure if she'd heard him say the word, but after church on Sunday, she found out that Noah had borrowed a Bible from Peter.

As Noah dug into the delicious food, he said, "I've been thinking that we need a project to do together and I came up with the perfect one."

Laura took a drink of her ice water. "What?" The twinkle in his eyes made her wary.

"A tree fort."

"A tree fort? What made you think of that?"

He lowered his gaze for a few seconds. "Because I always wanted a real one as a child, especially after my father tore down my pitiful attempt at one. When we get back to the house, I'll show you the plans I got off the Internet. I went by the hardware store and purchased the building materials. They'll deliver them tomorrow afternoon. Then we can start."

Beneath his adult exterior she saw a child lurking. "Then you've been thinking about this for a while."

"For a couple of weeks. I used to do some construction work as one of my jobs in college. I think I've worked out all my concerns for safety." He pointed toward a large coral tree, halfway between the gazebo and the pool area. "I'll build it independently of the tree. It will be a part of it, but the wooden support posts will be sunk in cement, so it won't put a strain on the trunk and branches. I'll use wood with a hard grade."

"How long is this going to take?" *Won't we be gone before you complete it?* was the question she really wanted to ask.

"If the weather cooperates and the kids help, we can have it done in a month or less." Excitement built in his voice and spilled over into his expression.

"I know Timothy will. He loves climbing trees and has never had something like that."

"Exactly. What child wouldn't like it?"

"And what adult?" she said with a laugh.

"Actually what I have in mind could serve as an adult retreat, too."

"You are thinking ahead."

"From what Children's Protective Service told me today, the kids may be here until school starts in August. Do you mind staying that long?"

"Do you mind them staying that long?"

He concentrated on cutting his ham into bite-size pieces. "No." A long pause and a deep breath later, he continued, "When you mentioned why the children had planned this little dinner, it got me thinking. I like you a lot." He stared into her eyes. "We could marry to give them a home. It's not that bad an idea. They need two parents. I didn't realize how important that is until I lived with Paul and Alice."

His half-baked marriage proposal knifed into her breaking heart. She would never marry for the wrong reason again. She would never marry another man unless she loved him and he loved her. No matter how tempting the idea was. Marriage to Noah certainly would solve some of her problems and make her son happy, but it would also produce a whole new set of troubles. How could she be around Noah, married to him, and know he didn't love her while she loved him? That very situation had destroyed her first marriage.

"Are you serious?" she finally asked, aware of his silent inquiry.

"Yes. The children have been here for almost two months and I find myself looking forward to coming home. I'm not spending as much time at work, but that's okay." He laughed. "I can't believe I just said that. But it's true. I have a well-organized business with good people in place to help me run it, so it's been all right for me to cut back my hours. Before, I used to work long hours to keep from coming home and wandering around the house trying to find things to do."

"With kids in the house, there's always something that needs to be done."

"I'm discovering that. So what do you think about us marrying to provide a home for them?" Noah slid a forkful of potato salad into his mouth.

"Although I think it's noble to want to give the children a home with both a father and a mother, I can't marry for any reason other than love. If the two parents don't love each other, the kids know and it affects them."

For a split second, disappointment invaded his gaze,

but he quickly blanked his expression. "I certainly understand that. It was a crazy idea and that's why I don't usually do things on the spur of the moment." He took a bite of his ham and chewed it. "Would you consider being my housekeeper permanently then? I could take the kids in, but I would need help."

The offer tempted her, but she had reservations—the main one being her feelings for Noah. How could she work for him on a long-term basis when she was in love with him? She didn't know if she could, even to give the children a home. "Let me think about that."

"Fine. I know it wasn't what you had intended when you agreed to this job."

Falling in love definitely wasn't what she had expected. Now she had to figure out what she needed to do for herself and Timothy.

Noah stared at the set of initials in the concrete that had dried, permanently preserving the letters *R J* for Rusty Johnson. The boy had left his mark more on his heart than on the mini basketball court he had made near where the tree house would be. With Rusty he had an opportunity to change a child's life, a child who was a lot like him growing up. Noah hadn't been able to alter his past, but Rusty's life could be different.

Noah tested the poles set in the concrete to make sure they were firmly in place. "We're ready for the next phase of Operation Tree Fort," he announced to the group standing behind him.

"Can I try the swing?" Lindsay danced around Cara.

"Me, too." Timothy raced for one of two swings attached to a beam behind the basketball goal and grabbed on before Lindsay.

"Sure, why not?" Noah said as the two kids pumped their legs to go higher.

"You've got to be quick with your answers." Cara came up to his side.

"We'll try this out. Make sure the net is set up right." Adam, who just happened to have a basketball with him, limped toward the small fourteen-foot by ten-foot court. "C'mon, Rusty. You can help me."

"I think you've lost your workers," Cara said with amusement in her voice.

Noah scratched his head. "This isn't turning out to be the family project I envisioned."

"Hey, Adam and I helped you some. There wasn't too much the younger kids could do about pouring concrete and putting in the support posts," Cara said.

"True." Noah unrolled the blueprint for the play platform and clubhouse, which would sit on top of the poles. "I thought we would start with the flooring today, then—" His cell ringing interrupted him.

Handing the design to Cara, Noah withdrew his phone, saw it was his private investigator, and answered it.

"Mr. Maxwell, I found your sister."

Chapter Ten

"You found Whitney!" Surprise registered on Noah's face as he turned away from Cara and walked toward the pool. The children's playful voices drowned out Noah's as he moved farther away.

Cara watched Timothy and Lindsay force their swings higher until she had to say, "That's high enough, you two."

"Ah, Mom, it was just getting fun. Test pilots see how fast the plane can go. We need to see how high the swings can go."

"That's not a plane and you're not a test pilot. Take it down a notch *now*."

Lindsay slowed down, but Timothy kept going.

"Young man!" Cara took a step toward him.

"Okay. A guy can't have any fun," Timothy mumbled.

Cara glanced over her shoulder at Noah. He snapped his cell closed and stuck it into his jean pocket. His shoulders hunched, he hung his head and stared at the ground near his feet.

He found his sister, and yet his body language didn't

convey the excitement she'd expected him to exhibit. Something was very wrong.

Cara crossed the yard to Noah. "Good news?"

"Whitney is living in Dallas, only three hours away."

"That's great! Are you going down there?"

Noah moved toward a chaise lounge near the pool and eased down on it. "Yes." He peered away for a long moment, then reestablished eye contact with her. "She works as a bartender. She lives in a tough part of town."

Cara sat across from him. By his tone she knew he had left something out, something he was wrestling with. "I know how you feel about alcohol and drinking, but that doesn't mean she drinks what she serves."

Taking a deep breath, he closed his eyes for a few seconds. "The private investigator told me she is a bit rough around the edges. Apparently from what he has discovered, Whitney hasn't had an easy life so far." He offered her a self-mocking smile. "I realize now that when I thought about my little sister I always pictured her as I last saw her—eight years old, innocent in spite of what she had lived through and trusting I would take care of her."

Rusty's cheers intruded. Cara glanced at the basketball court and saw him shoot at the hoop and make it. Another yell of triumph went up, and Adam gave his brother a high five.

"When are you going to Dallas?"

"Tomorrow. I shouldn't put it off." Uncertainty dimmed the light in Noah's eyes.

"Do you want me to ride with you? I can keep you company until you meet her."

Relief rippled through his expression, leaving a half grin in place. "I would love some company. To tell you the truth, I don't know what to say to her. I never stopped to think about that since I've spent years looking for her." He shrugged. "I guess I thought I would never find her."

"Does she go by Whitney Maxwell?"

"No, Dawn Burnett. The last name of the people who adopted her was Coleman. I don't know why she's going by Burnett. Dawn was her middle name. She hated it so it's strange she's calling herself that now."

"That was over twenty years ago. Maybe she grew to love it."

Noah shook his head. "No, I think something is terribly wrong. We'd been following this elusive trail for years. Just when I thought we would finally find her, she would disappear. I think she's hiding or running away from someone, but I don't know who."

Cara reached out and took Noah's hand. It trembled within her grasp. "Then we definitely need to go tomorrow before she disappears again. Then you'll learn the truth of what happened to your sister. No more guessing."

He stared long and hard into her gaze. "Perhaps. You're right. It's been over twenty years and I'm sure she has changed."

"I'll ask Laura if we can drop the kids off at her place tomorrow. I'm sure she wouldn't mind getting them to school and watching them afterward until we return to Cimarron City."

He covered their clasped hands. "Thanks for coming with me."

"What are friends for? I'm here to help where I can. Besides, it will take my mind off the trial starting in a few days."

"I'm glad it's finally here."

"Yeah, especially for Adam's sake. He told me a couple of guys at school on the baseball team found out he'll be a witness and said a few things to him."

"Why didn't he tell me?"

Cara spied Adam lining up for a shot in front of the net. "Because he didn't want you to go up to the school. He took care of it."

"How?"

"He walked away."

Noah rubbed his finger along the back of hers. "The truth will come out about those three, and all this commotion surrounding them and us will disappear."

"I hope so, Noah. The assistant D.A. thinks the trial should only be two days at the most. With it starting Thursday, it should be over by the weekend."

He rose and pulled her to her feet, inches from him. "Although we know what really happened, are you prepared if the truth doesn't triumph?"

"If they are found not guilty? Yes, I am…" She tried to draw air into her oxygen-deprived lungs, but she couldn't seem to fill them. "No, I'm not. I still believe in the system, that the guilty are found guilty and the innocent are freed."

"Even if they are found guilty, they may only get a minimum sentence, a token fine."

"I have to put it in God's hands. I can't control the actions of others, only myself."

Noah brushed her hair behind her ears, a gentle look caressing her. "Those are words to live by."

"Which ones?"

"Both sentences."

Did he believe in the Lord? "What are you saying?" Cara held her breath while seconds ticked off.

"I'm coming to the conclusion I can't always control my life, even though I've tried hard over these past twenty years. Maybe it's time I put it in God's hands."

"Do you mean that?"

One side of his mouth hitched up. "I'm working on it. I've been reading a Bible I borrowed from Peter every night before I go to bed. I do have questions—"

"Mom! Look at this," Timothy called out.

As Cara peered toward her son, she said to Noah, "Hold those questions until tomorrow. We'll have three hours to talk uninterrupted."

Timothy flew off the swing, sailing through the air. Landing with a thud, he collapsed to the ground, groaning.

"Oh, no!" Cara raced toward her son, picturing another broken limb.

"I think Laura's twins definitely are having a bad influence on Timothy. He never was a daredevil before coming to Cimarron City." Cara shifted in the passenger seat of Noah's Corvette, trying to get comfortable after spending two and a half hours sitting in the car as they headed toward Dallas.

Noah tossed her a wry grin. "At least he didn't break anything."

"This time. The odds are he will if he keeps doing that kind of stuff. Did you see Lindsay start to do it?"

"Thankfully your scream paralyzed her."

"It's the ripple-down effect. I'm gonna have to have a word with the twins."

"Boys will be boys," he said with a chuckle.

"Did you ever do things like jump from the roof of a house or try to fly through the air?"

His expression sobered. "Probably. I try not to think about my childhood, but I suppose I need to since we're going to meet an important part of that childhood."

"Your sister. How much younger is she?"

"Six years. The last time I saw her she was almost eight."

"I wonder why she didn't try to find you when she got old enough."

The line of his jaw hardened. "I let her down."

Cara turned so she faced him. "How?"

"I wasn't able to protect like I should have."

"Wasn't that your father's job, not yours?"

"Should have been but not in our household. I was all she had besides our dad once our mother left after Whitney's birth."

"Did you ever try to find your mother?"

"Yes. She died fifteen years ago. I never got to talk to her again, but maybe that was for the better. She didn't want us or she would have taken us with her when she left."

Cara stared out the windshield. The landscape changed from open spaces to the start of the small towns that surrounded Dallas. "My parents might have been overprotective, but I always knew they loved me."

"Overprotective? How?"

"I didn't date much in high school. My senior year they gave me more leeway, but I led a pretty sheltered life when it came to boys." *And that cost me dearly in the end,* Cara added silently.

Noah slowed as the traffic became heavier on the outskirts of Dallas. "I had a parent who didn't care what I did and you had one who cared too much. How in the world does a parent know what the right balance is?"

"Practice. I also think it's important to listen to your child. Communication is so crucial."

For the next few miles Noah concentrated on the cars around them and didn't say anything. Finally he broke the silence with, "Is it really true the way to salvation is through Jesus Christ?"

"It's the only way. He died for us and our sins."

"So all we have to do is believe in Jesus and God forgives us our sins."

"If you repent."

"Even if you did something awful?"

"Yes. The Bible is full of stories of God's forgiveness. One of the disciples was Saul. Before his conversion he was instrumental in trying to destroy the disciples and their spreading of the good news. Jesus chose him to carry His name to the Gentiles."

"Amazing." Noah took an exit into the heart of the city.

Silence fell again while he negotiated the streets. The area they entered was seedy—run-down houses with overgrown yards and trash piled high on several porches.

"I want to try where she lives first. I doubt she's working this early."

"Does she know you're coming?"

He shook his head. "I'm afraid she'll run." Fear roughened his voice.

Cara hurt for Noah. No wonder he had never wanted a family. His experience being a part of one hadn't been good. She sent up a prayer that all would go well with his reunion with his sister.

He pulled up to an apartment complex that hadn't seen the landlord's kind hand in a while. Peeling paint and several boarded up windows as well as foot-high grass and weeds spoke of the lack of care.

"This is it." He switched off the engine and sat behind the steering wheel with his grip white-knuckle.

"Do you want me to come with you or wait out here?"

He scanned the area. "Definitely come with me. This doesn't look too safe. I don't want you waiting out in the car."

"Fine. I'll hang back. You won't even notice me."

His chuckle came out forced. "Sorry, that would be kinda hard for me." His look pinned her to the cushion, his eyes warm with appreciation as they skimmed over her features. "Just in case I haven't told you enough, thanks for coming with me."

"You're welcome. I enjoyed the drive." *The time spent with you.*

He blew out a deep breath. "I guess I'm as ready as I ever will be."

She'd never seen Noah so tentative. He was always so self-assured and capable. The vulnerability she'd glimpsed occasionally in the past had come to the foreground as he pushed open his door and exited his car. He quickly rounded the front and waited for her to join him.

Inside the three-story building he examined the mailboxes and found the one with the name Dawn Burnett on it. He glanced toward the stairs and gestured for her to go first.

As he followed her up the steps, a musky, stale odor assailed her nostrils. A baby wailing echoed down the hallway on the third floor. Noah paused in front of the door to his sister's apartment, lifting his fist to knock. Suddenly he dropped his arm back to his side.

"Noah?"

"I've dreamed and anticipated this moment for years. I'm not sure I'm ready."

"We can leave and come back a little later if you need more time."

"Yes." He turned toward her and started to walk away. In midstride he stopped. "No, it won't be any easier an hour from now." Back at the door, Noah pounded it. The sound of a television wafted through the wood.

"Someone must be home." Cara stood slightly to the side and behind him.

Noah knocked again.

"What do you want?" came a deep throaty woman's voice from the other side.

"I'm looking for Wh—Dawn Burnett."

"She isn't here."

Noah stiffened. "When will she be back?"

"Don't know."

His gaze, full of anguish, connected with Cara's. "Are you her roommate?"

"Go away or I'll call the police."

Cara's heart throbbed at the bleak look on Noah's face. He'd searched for so long, only for his sister still to be out of reach. She gripped his hand.

"I'm dialing right now."

He glanced back at the closed door, as though it was an impregnable barrier, and Cara supposed it was in that moment. She tugged him toward her, nodding with her head at the staircase. He trudged down the steps to the first floor and stopped in front of the bank of mailboxes.

"Do you think that was Whitney?"

His voice held such sadness that its sound speared Cara. Vulnerable, his emotions exposed, he closed his eyes for a few seconds, their hands still linked.

"Noah, I don't know. It could have been a roommate, but the P.I. told you she lived alone."

"Yeah, that's why I think it was her."

"Then why didn't you tell her who you were?"

His gaze swerved to hers. "Because I'm afraid then she wouldn't have opened the door for sure. There was a peek hole. She saw who I was."

"But the last time you saw her she was eight and you were fourteen."

"Still I've lived in Cimarron City all my life. I just now started wondering why she didn't come back and look me up. I never changed my name."

"You think she blames you for what happened to her?"

"Yes."

"Then what are you going to do?"

"Wait and go to where she works later today." He faced her, taking both of her hands in his. "Do you mind staying in Dallas for a while? Do you think Laura would watch the kids until we get home late tonight?"

"No to both questions. I'll call her and let her know we won't be home until later."

"Great." He attempted a smile that failed.

She wanted so badly to touch the corners of his mouth as though her caress could will him to grin. Instead, she tightened her hold, trying to convey her support through that physical contact. "What do you want to do until we go to her work?"

"Watch the building. I don't want her to decide to run. One way or another this needs to be settled tonight."

Noah stepped inside the dark, smoke-filled bar and hated the fact that Cara had to be here in a place like this. For that matter, he hated that Whitney did. The smell of beer and cigarettes brought back horrendous memories of his father. Bile rose in his throat.

As it had throughout the day, Cara's presence gave him the courage to proceed into the dim interior. He searched the large room with only a few people sitting about at tables and found his sister behind the long bar at the far end. The photo the private investigator had taken for him hadn't done her justice. Beneath the heavy makeup was a beautiful woman, but there was a harsh edge to her manner and bearing, he noticed as he paused and watched her interact with a customer.

Whitney leaned toward the older man and listened to something he said to her, then she tossed back her head and laughed, an abrasive sound that came across forced. Noah moved to a stool and eased down while Cara took the one next to him.

His sister turned from the customer and spied him. Her eyes flared then narrowed on him. With mouth set firmly, she advanced toward him.

"I can call the police just as easily from here as at home. You aren't welcome in here."

"May I have a soda?" Cara asked, pulling Whitney's attention toward her. "I'm thirsty."

His sister looked Cara up and down. "There's a restaurant down the street. I'm sure you can get a soda there."

"You don't serve nonalcoholic beverages in here?"

"This is a bar, in case you haven't figured it out." Anger threaded each word and vibrated down Whitney's length. She swung her full attention back to him. "I don't appreciate being stalked. I have friends in here who can take care of you if you don't leave now."

"You don't recognize me, Whitney."

Shock forced the anger to the side. "My name is Dawn Burnett."

"But you were born Whitney Dawn Maxwell. I'm Noah Maxwell, your brother."

All the color drained from her face. His sister backed

away, her hands trembling. “Burt, this man is causing trouble,” she finally yelled, but her voice broke on the last word.

A huge man, sitting at a table in a dimly lit corner, stood and lumbered toward them. “Time to leave.”

Noah rose. “I am not leaving until my sister and I talk.”

“Sister?” Burt peered at Whitney. “I don’t want to get into the middle of a family dispute.” He raised his hands and took several steps back.

Whitney started to say something, but Noah spun around. “I’m not leaving until we talk. I’ve been searching for you for years. You should remember I don’t give up easily.”

“You’ve been looking for me?” His sister’s forehead creased, her mouth set in a thoughtful expression. She surveyed the room. “It’s quiet right now. Let’s go over there.”

“I’ll stay here,” Cara said to Noah. “And I really would like at least a glass of water.”

Whitney picked up a tumbler and filled it with ice, then water. After placing it on the counter in front of Cara, Whitney came from behind the bar and went the few short steps to a table off to the side.

“I may have to get up and serve a customer.” She sat across from him, her body held rigidly as though she would break at any moment. Wariness settled into her eyes as she faced him. “Why are you here?”

“We’re family. The only one we have.”

“Family doesn’t mean much to me.” She lifted her thin shoulders in a shrug. “Why should it?”

He’d said those words many times over the years. With a quick look at Cara, he leaned forward. “Because I’m discovering how important family is in life. At least the right one.”

The harsh line of her jaw greeted his answer. A pinpoint gaze zeroed in on him. "Right one? There is such a thing?"

"Yes." He let the answer hang in the air between them for a brief moment. "Lately I've had the good fortune to have been exposed to what a family can really be like."

"I'm thrilled for you," she said with deep sarcasm.

He cringed. What had happened to his little sister to make her feel that way, to be so bitter? He was at a lost on how to proceed with Whitney. *Lord, what do I do?*

"What do you want from me?" She chewed on her bottom lip.

"I want us to be a family again, to get to know each other."

She pulled herself up even straighter. "I'm fine the way things are in my life right now. I see no reason to change anything."

"So you enjoy bartending."

She thrust herself forward, her balled hands on the table. "It pays the bills most of the time."

Noah took a deep breath. "I would think after what our dad did to us you wouldn't want to have anything to do with drinking or people who get drunk."

His sister shot to her feet. "This conversation is over. We've talked so now leave. Or are you a man who doesn't keep his word?"

He slowly stood, realizing he had handled the whole situation wrong. He knew better than to judge because he recognized all the defensive tactics she was using. He'd used them himself. He'd gotten quite good at pushing others away—until Cara. He glanced toward her. Somehow she had burrowed her way past his defenses. Could he do the same with Whitney?

His sister whirled around and marched back to the bar where she kept herself occupied wiping down the clean counter. He withdrew a business card and wrote his personal contact information on the back.

He walked to his sister. "Whitney—"

"Don't call me that. I'm Dawn. That person died a long time ago." She clenched the rag she held.

"This is my phone number and address. Please contact me anytime you need to talk or need help. I'm here for you. I'm just sorry it took me so long to find you."

She stared down at the card, then crumpled it into a wad and tossed it to the floor. "I don't need your help or anyone else's. I take care of myself."

"I used to think that, too. I was wrong. It's mighty lonely."

She pivoted away from him, muttering, "Lonely is better than the alternative."

Noah sighed, his sister's ramrod-straight back emphasizing her position more than words. He wouldn't get through tonight, perhaps never, but he would keep trying even if he had to travel to Dallas every week.

Making his way to Cara, he tried to maintain a smile but the corners of his mouth quivered. "Ready to leave?"

"Are you?"

"I don't have a choice. I told her I would if we talked."

Cara slid from the stool and walked toward the door. "Were you successful at all?"

"You saw her toss my card on the floor. I would say no." Stepping outside, Noah inhaled the fresh air. "We should roll down the window on the way back to Cimarron City. Nothing's worse than smelling cigarette smoke clinging to our clothes. My father smoked and, growing up, I always hated that smell almost as much as alcohol."

At his car Cara settled into the passenger seat, staring at the neon sign that proclaimed the place was a bar. "What are you going to do now?"

"Go home. Boy, does that sound good right now." He slipped his hand over hers. "My place was never a home until lately. Thanks."

"I haven't done anything."

"You've helped me look at my situation differently. I've always been so focused on going a mile a minute. I never allowed myself to stop much. Now I see how important it is to take some time off and enjoy the simple things."

"I thought you worked hard and played hard."

He chuckled. "You see I didn't even know how to relax while I was playing."

Cara glanced at the clock on the dashboard. "I'm glad Laura decided to watch the children at your house. We won't get back until midnight. This way they will be asleep and we won't have to wake them up." With a sigh, she leaned her head back. "It's been a long day."

"Yeah," Noah started the engine, "I never knew a stakeout could be so much work." He threw her a smile she probably didn't see in the dark. "I'm glad you came along. I had fun in spite of the long hours sitting in the same spot."

"We could have traded places. You should have said something." Laughter tinged her voice.

He drove out of the parking lot next to the bar. "You have to understand that could have been pure torture to a man who is always on the go, but your scintillating conversation was music to my ears."

"Then I'm glad I could help."

The streetlight cast her face in a soft glow. Every day

she grew more beautiful in his mind. There was nothing plain about her. Her eyes sparkled with life. Her lustrous hair lured a person to run his fingers through the strands. Her mouth—he refused to think about that or he would pull over and kiss her.

By the time he reached the highway and pointed his Corvette north, Cara slumped against the window, asleep. The occasional headlights shone across her peaceful features. Although he would love to have her company on the three-hour trip back to Cimarron City, he couldn't disturb her rest, especially with the trial coming up on Thursday. She hadn't said anything on the drive down to Dallas, but he knew how bothered she was with all the negative publicity. He had become very good at tuning out others; she hadn't. Each hurtful comment found its mark. He did his best to shield her, but the outside world leaked through the screen he had around her.

Lord, I'm new at this praying. I'm not sure how to do it, but please protect Cara from being hurt at the trial. Make these guys pay for what they did to her.

Chapter Eleven

The evening before the trial, Noah swept his arm toward the tree house. "We have a floor, Houston."

Cara couldn't believe the elaborate construction that they had been working on for almost a week. Noah was getting into it more than even Rusty and Timothy.

Lindsay screwed her face into a puzzled look. "Who's Houston?"

Adam scooped his little sister up into his arms. "With all the TV you've watched, I would have thought you'd know, Lindy. Houston is where the Space Center is." He swung her up. "Hey, I think you've gained some weight."

The little girl giggled. "Cara's a good cook."

Adam set Lindsay on the ground. "I'm wounded you think Cara cooks better than me."

"Is that what you called heating up a pizza or pouring cereal and milk into a bowl?" Rusty put his arm around Lindsay's shoulder. "We're here to tell you that you can't cook."

Cara backed away, her heart heavy. Noah had been right about building the tree house. Over this past week everyone had come together as a family—although they really weren't one. In order to keep the three siblings together, she saw Noah coming to the conclusion he could be a foster parent by himself, especially after his meeting with his sister two days ago. Her time would be over soon, and she and Timothy would leave Noah's house, possibly even Cimarron City.

Adam thumped his cast. "Just because I have this on doesn't mean I can't wrestle you to the ground. And wait until I get it removed next week. Then you better really watch out."

"Oh, I'm scared." Rusty stepped back. "It's kinda hard running in that cast."

A mockingly stern expression descended on Adam's face. "Where there's a will, there's a way. Just try me. I can run rings around you."

Rusty stuck his tongue out and put his fingers into his ears, taunting his older brother. Prancing about, he said, "In your dreams."

Adam charged past Lindsay, who shrieked. He went after Rusty. The nine-year-old scampered toward the gazebo, halfway there turning around and jogging backward. With determination on his face, Adam kept hobbling toward his younger brother.

"Remind me to give Dr. McCoy a bonus next time Rusty goes to see him." Noah's whispered words flowed over Cara's ear.

She shivered. "The changes in Rusty haven't only been because of his therapist. You have made a big difference. Did you see his big grin when you showed him how to nail those boards for the floor?"

"Yeah. For a few seconds I think I know what Peter

and Jacob feel like when they are with their kids. Not a bad feeling."

"No." Her heart pitterpattered. He was much too near for her peace of mind. "Those are the moments you cherish and pull out when they are doing something wrong."

"You mean they aren't gonna be perfect from now on?"

A yell for help from the gazebo answered his question. She gestured toward Adam, who managed somehow to catch up with Rusty and get him on the ground. Her son raced toward his friend and jumped on Adam's back, then both boys ganged up on the teen.

"Good thing his cast is coming off on Monday. Should I step in?" Noah started forward.

"Hi, boss."

He stopped and turned toward Lisa coming around from the front of the house with several large pizza boxes. "I've got a better idea. Lindsay, go tell your brothers and Timothy dinner is here and I'm starved so if they want any pizza they better hurry."

Lisa set the boxes on the table by the pool and strolled toward the coral tree. "I couldn't resist coming out here and seeing the fort you told us about. Andy would love something like that, especially the slide."

"Your son is welcome to come visit anytime. I thought the kids would enjoy having more than one way to leave the tree house." Noah escorted his employee to the bottom of the structure and described what he was going to have when it was finished.

Cara made her way to the glass table and opened the boxes. The scents of onion, green pepper, meat, tomato, bread and various spices swamped her, teasing her empty stomach. She lifted up a piece and gave it to her son, who came to a skidding halt at her elbow.

"The sodas are in the ice chest on the basketball court." Although the food smelled wonderful, Cara couldn't bring herself to eat.

The children dug in and wolfed down several slices before Noah finished with Lisa. When his employee left, Cara retrieved two bottled waters from the cooler and passed one to Noah.

"Aren't you hungry? Water won't go far." Noah selected a slice of pizza with the works.

"Haven't you heard you should fill up on water before you eat and you won't eat as much?"

"Is that what you're doing? Or is it because you're testifying tomorrow at the trial?"

She moved away from the children. She didn't want them to overhear. "So are you and Adam."

"We have truth on our sides."

"I know, but when the assistant D.A. went over my testimony yesterday, he prepped me on some of the tactics the defense attorney may use. I don't like confrontation. I always went out of my way to avoid it."

"I'll be there. So will Adam. When you get upset or nervous, just look at us."

"I don't think the D.A. wants me to start laughing."

"Cute. If you don't watch out, I'll take pointers from Rusty and stick my tongue out and wave my fingers."

"That's mine." Rusty tugged a slice from Lindsay's hand. "That's my favorite kind."

"Excuse me, Cara. I'll be right back." Noah jogged over to the two kids playing tug-of-war with a piece of pizza.

Needing some alone time, she strolled toward the

gazebo and sat on one of the cushion seats along the perimeter. She stared toward the pond, trying to wash her mind of all thoughts concerning tomorrow.

She was glad the protesters weren't at the restaurant anymore. From Lisa she'd learned that Noah's business had suffered because of the trial, though. Yes, it was starting to pick up, but the bad week had hurt Noah financially. She'd seen it in the tired lines about his eyes and his occasional faraway look. When she had heard him talking to Peter and Jacob about it, he hadn't fooled her with his bravado.

Staring at the family of geese that had joined the ducks on the pond, she folded her arms along the railing and rested her chin on them. Noah had given her so much—everything she needed, except his love.

Footsteps coming up the stairs into the gazebo alerted her to Noah's arrival. His presence brought back memories of the dinner the children had surprised them with only a week ago. In that time so much had happened.

Noah slipped in next to her on the seat. He brushed her hair behind her ear, his touch whisper soft.

"Who got the pizza?"

"I did."

Cara laughed and lifted her head, angling around toward him. "So instead of one child being happy and one unhappy, you got two who aren't pleased."

"Yep. The pizza was good if I do say so myself."

"Even though it was a little worse for wear?"

"Do you know they are finding certain germs are good for us?"

"You are a wealth of trivia."

"Look who's talking, the lady who told me about drinking water right before dinner so I'd eat less."

"That was in case you ever wanted to go on a diet."

His eyes twinkled. "Which won't be long with your good cooking."

He wouldn't have to eat her food too much longer. The children should be settled in their foster home, whether it was with Noah or not, before school started. At least she hoped so.

"Have I successfully taken your mind off tomorrow?"

She checked her watch. "Yeah, up until two seconds ago."

"Okay, I'm not very good at this."

"At what?"

"Helping someone through a problem."

"You don't give yourself enough credit. You do a very good job." She lifted one of her eyebrows. "Well, usually."

"Just think, this time tomorrow evening it will be over with. Keep that in mind." He took her hand nearest him and cupped it between his large ones. "Let's meet back here tomorrow night at sundown. We can have our own celebration."

"I'll be ready to put those guys behind me. I've even come to accept that very likely nothing will happen to them. Like those 'sweep under the rug' public intoxication charges."

"We don't know that yet."

"You don't think those protesters didn't sway a few people to their way of thinking?"

"I'm hoping not, but if so, you and I, God and they know what really happened." He rubbed her hand between his. "One good thing is that the D.A. thinks the trial will go quickly. We might know the verdict by the end of the day."

"Have you ever feared and hoped for something at the same time? That's how I feel about tomorrow."

"I called Whitney today before she went to work. I wanted to emphasize that I am here for her."

"Did she talk to you?"

"Not much." A lopsided grin appeared on his face. "She did listen for a few minutes before she hung up. I call that progress."

"Give her time."

He rose. "Come on. You need to eat something." Tugging her to her feet, he pressed her against him.

"You've become a regular mother hen."

He laughed, the deep belly kind. "That isn't a pretty picture in my mind."

He smoothed her hair back, his gaze bound to hers. Slowly he lowered his head toward hers, his eyes flaring.

"Mom! Noah! It's almost dark and the stars are gonna be out soon."

Cara stepped away quickly, her mouth still tingling in anticipation of the kiss she knew he would have given her if it hadn't been for her son and Rusty clambering into the gazebo. "My son the astronomer. You would think he'd just discovered stars come out at night."

"Is this another aspect of being a parent, being interrupted at the most inconvenient times?" He touched his forehead to hers.

"Afraid so."

"C'mon, you guys. We should be able to see Mars tonight." Rusty stood by the entrance.

"I promised them I would get out my telescope and we would look through it tonight."

"What telescope?"

Mischief graced his grin. "The one I purchased today."

She turned toward the boys, who tapped their feet against the wooden floor. "You are spoiling them," she said out of the side of her mouth.

"Is that part of being a parent?"

"No, that's a grandparent's job."

"Oh, I got confused."

"Yeah, right." She crossed to Rusty and Timothy. "You say we might get to see Mars. How about the man in the moon?"

Timothy giggled. "Mom, there can't be a man living in the moon. It's made out of cheese."

"Then a mouse in the moon."

Rusty and Timothy raced toward the house, their laughter drifting to her.

"You've made two little boys very happy."

Noah stopped at the bottom of the gazebo's steps. "Just two little boys?"

"Well, probably a little girl and a teen, too."

Noah peered over his shoulder toward the boys, then yanked her to him. Before she had time to catch her breath, he planted a hard kiss on her mouth that quickly evolved into one that stole her heart.

"Only the children?" he whispered in the gray dimness right before the sun went down.

"Okay, maybe one tired and hungry housekeeper."

He slipped his arm around her. "Good. Let's get you something to eat then look at the stars together. Maybe the children will go to bed early. It is a school night."

"It is official. We managed to wear the kids out." Noah came out onto the deck, gazing up at the sky. "It was a beautiful night to look at the stars."

"So Lindsay and Rusty went to bed without any problem?" Cara slipped on her sweater she had brought back with her from the guesthouse after putting Timothy down.

"Yep. Lindsay was asleep when her head hit the

pillow. Rusty held out for a whole two minutes. How about Timothy?"

"The same. I barely got him back to the cottage before he started nodding off. It's not easy undressing a child standing up when they are trying to go to sleep."

"You don't have to help me clean up if you're tired."

"I don't think I'm gonna sleep a wink tonight."

He took her by the arms and waited until he had her full attention before saying, "You are not to think about the trial one more second. Don't let them have that kind of power over you."

"Yes, sir. I'd salute but you have my arms trapped."

He dropped his hands away. "Go right ahead. I'm glad you know who is in charge."

"I'm just letting you think you are."

"I know." He leaned back against the railing. "This morning I went by a car dealership."

His sports car was a symbol of his way of life to him. "Don't tell me you're thinking of trading in your Corvette?"

"Not exactly trading it in. I thought I would buy an SUV and have two cars."

"An SUV!" Stunned, she lounged back next to him, staring at the French doors and the great room beyond. "That's something I would like to see, you driving a soccer mom's car."

"Are you making fun of me?"

Pressing her lips together, she nodded.

"And here I thought I could tell you anything. You have crushed my faith in the human race." He projected hurt into his voice, but a grin graced his mouth.

She jabbed him playfully in the ribs. "It would take more than that. You are one of the strongest people I've known."

He pushed from the railing and bowed. "Thank you, ma'am."

"I wish I had your strength, then tomorrow wouldn't bother me."

As his gaze reestablished eye contact with her, his expression sobered. "I thought we decided we wouldn't talk about the trial."

"You decided. I'm not sure I can just dismiss it like that." Cara snapped her fingers.

He captured her hand and drew her toward him. "I am not as strong as you think. I'm just very good at hiding my feelings behind this." He gestured toward his face.

"How did you get that way? I wish I didn't wear my emotions for everyone to see."

"I wouldn't change anything about you."

"That's sweet. You're too kind."

"I've never been described as sweet," he said with a self-mocking laugh. "It took some hard life lessons to get the way I am."

"I was fortunate to have loving parents. You didn't. That would affect anyone."

"It's much more than that, Cara. I've done some things that I'm not proud of. I've spent the last years trying to make up for those mistakes, but guess what? You can't really run from the truth, your past."

His words twisted her stomach. She knew that more than most. But for Timothy's sake she was determined to keep her past in the past. She never wanted her son to be hurt by it. "Having a father who abused you isn't your fault. Even what happened concerning your separation from your sister isn't your fault."

"Yes, it was."

She gripped his upper arms. "No, it wasn't. You can't

always fight the system. You were fourteen. Some things are out of your control."

"How well I'm finding that out. But you're wrong, Cara. It was my fault because until the family who adopted Whitney found out about my troubles they had been willing to adopt me, too."

"What troubles?"

He pulled back and put some distance between them. "Mostly fighting. I was so angry at my dad but could never do anything about that until…" He turned away.

"Until?" The anguish in his tone shoved her concerns about the trial to the background.

For a long moment he didn't reply. Cara wanted to hold him, erase the pain, but his inflexible stance forbade it.

"Until at thirteen I was big enough to stand up to my father," Noah said in a raw voice. "I nearly killed him." He pivoted, his arms rigid at his sides. "He was beating on Whitney and I couldn't let him do that. It was one thing to hit me, but not her."

Her heart bled for him. What he must have gone through. She came toward him.

He put his hand up, halting her halfway to him. "I don't want your pity. I was wrong. If my sister hadn't stopped me, I would have killed my father. I have to live with that." A merciless laugh erupted from deep in him. "You would have thought I would have learned not to fight. I continued trying to solve all my problems by striking out at whoever caused them. It wasn't until I went to live with Paul and Alice that I began to change, slowly, reluctantly."

She didn't care he didn't want her near him. She covered the space in a few strides but didn't touch him.

"In fact, the Hendersons were my last chance before

juvenile detention. Somehow they got through to me and didn't give up on me."

He looked directly into her eyes, and somehow even with all that he had revealed, his expression didn't hint at what was going on inside him.

"I found it was easier to control myself by shutting down my feelings. It usually worked for me until I met you. If I had known what those guys were trying to do to you in the parking lot, I would have fought them in order to save you. I came close with them in the restaurant. That would have been the first time in almost twenty years."

"Oh, Noah, I'm sorry." She finally laid her hand on his arm. The tension beneath her fingertips conveyed how upset he was, but little showed in his expression. He clung desperately to old habits.

"Don't you see? There's something about you that makes me want to lose control, to let everything out. I've never told anyone this. Never, not even the Hendersons, Jacob or Peter. But here I am, telling you. I don't understand. What is it about you that does that to me?"

She didn't have an answer for him, but he wanted one. "I'm a good listener. I—I don't know." She shrugged. "I try never to judge another." The verse from John came to mind. "If any one of you is without sin, let him be the first to throw a stone at her." But she knew his fear because she had been on the other end, judged and condemned.

He framed her face with his hands. "I feel like I've been gutted." One corner of his mouth tilted upward. "No wonder I don't lay my soul bare every day."

She cupped her hands over his, tears glistening in her eyes. Through the sheen the most endearing look transformed his expression into an open one. She needed to share hers with him, but the words stuck in her throat.

Swallowing several times, she attempted a reassuring smile. "Even for someone like me, who wears her feelings on her sleeve, it's never easy. I—"

"Mom."

A wheezing sound punctuated the stillness and sent alarm down her. She whirled around.

Timothy mounted the last step. "I can't—" a series of coughs mingled with his gasps "—breathe."

Cara flew across the deck and gathered her son to her. "Let's get you back to the cottage."

She started to pick up Timothy, but Noah came around her and scooped him into his arms. She followed them down the stairs and across the pool area. Her heart galloped as it always did when her son had an asthma attack.

Noah shouldered his way into the guesthouse. "Where do you want me to put him?"

"The couch. I have to give him a breathing treatment." She headed into the small kitchen and retrieved Timothy's nebulizer.

Back in the living room her hands shook as she prepared the treatment for her son. His wheezing worsened as she gave him the hose. His pale face and continual coughing scared her. This was a bad attack.

"What if this doesn't work?" Noah's ashen features spoke of his own concern.

"Then I do another treatment, and if I don't think I can get it under control, we pay a visit to the doctor, or in this case, because it's in the middle of the night, the emergency room."

When two more sessions with the nebulizer didn't improve Timothy much, Cara looked at Noah. "Please watch him while I get my purse."

"I'm coming with you."

"You don't have to," she automatically said as she grabbed her bag with her car keys.

"Yes, I do. Give me a moment to let Adam know where we're going. I'm also calling Jacob. He can meet us at the hospital."

"I hate to disturb him. The E.R. doc—"

"Cara, I don't hate disturbing him. He's the best pediatrician in town. I'll feel better if he's there." Noah jogged from the cottage.

"Mom, I'm okay." Coughs perforated his raspy words.

She pulled him up next to her. "Hon, you will be."

Two minutes later, Noah rushed back into the cottage. "Let's go." Again he lifted the boy into his arms and headed out to Cara's car.

She gave him the keys while he settled Timothy in her lap. Noah's presence comforted her in ways she hadn't ever known with Tim. She wasn't alone in dealing with the asthma. In St. Louis she'd always felt she had been.

Father, please take care of my son. I'm the one who was wrong, not Timothy. Punish me, not him.

Chapter Twelve

Noah drove past the courthouse, his grip on the steering wheel tightening. A few protesters were out in front with those signs they loved to carry. He slid a glance toward Adam then Cara. As she looked away from them, her mouth firmed into a frown and her hands clenched in her lap.

"I'm sorry they are here," Noah said, at a loss for adequate words.

"You have nothing to be sorry for." Weariness infused her voice. "Hopefully this will be the last day we have to suffer them."

Noah pulled into the parking lot next to the building and found a space. "Stay close to me, you two. I'll handle them if they bother us."

"Fine," came her lackluster reply, which was out of character, heightening Noah's concern. Cara and he had been up most of the night with Timothy at the hospital. He'd managed to catch a few hours of sleep before getting ready for his court appearance, but he wondered if Cara had. When he'd left her early this morning, she'd been sitting by her son's bed, watching him, as though she was afraid to go to sleep in case he had another attack.

One of the protesters saw them walking toward the steps. "Ready for this?" Noah quickened his pace.

"No, but we don't have a choice." Even as tired as Cara was, she didn't drop her head or look down. She directed her gaze straight ahead, fixated on the double doors into the building.

Adam, even with his walking cast still on, managed to keep up with them.

A man yelled, "Liars."

Cara tensed, her step faltering. Adam halted, his hands balling.

"Ignore them. We know the truth. God knows the truth. That's all that's important." Noah took her hand to make sure she kept up with him.

Another person shouted something unrepeatable. Cara's cheeks colored.

"I can't believe these guys. We need to say something." The incredulous tone in Adam's voice reflected how Noah felt, but he knew confrontation on the courthouse steps wasn't the solution.

"A few more feet and we're home free." Noah held the door open for them and waited until they entered before following them inside. "The hard part is over with."

She shook her head. "I wish."

"At least Timothy is fine now. He's a trooper." Noah fit her hand within his again as he threw a look toward Adam to make sure he was keeping up. "He had me worried last night."

And you have me worried now. The deep circles under Cara's eyes, as though they were bruised, and her lethargic movements concerned him. Timothy had gotten his fighting spirit from his mother, but right now she was exhausted and seemed defeated, which made his apprehension multiply.

"Last night was a bad episode. Thanks for calling Jacob. I did feel better with him there at the hospital."

"Was it the first attack he's had since coming to Cimarron City?"

"He's had a few small ones, but the breathing treatment at home took care of it."

Noah slipped his touch to the small of her back as they entered the empty elevator to take to the second floor. "You never said anything."

"Both Timothy and I like to deal with it in a matter-of-fact manner. He doesn't even want people to know. My husband used to make him feel as though he had done something wrong."

"He did? Why?"

Cara didn't answer him. She came to a halt at the doors that led into the courtroom. Her gaze connected with his. "After this is over with, we need to talk."

The ominous words stunned him. He never liked it when someone said to him we need to talk. The muscles in his neck and shoulders constricted as he eased into the seat next to Cara on the front row right behind the assistant district attorney. Adam settled next to him on the other side.

The bailiff announced the entrance of the judge and they rose. Noah gripped Cara's hand, which trembled, and sent up a silent prayer for strength.

"Thank you, Mrs. Winters." Finished with his questions, the assistant district attorney took his seat behind the prosecutor's table.

The defense lawyer, his thin face and bald head out of place on his stocky body, rose slowly, checked his notes then proceeded toward Cara, a look of disdain on his face. "You want these good men and women of the jury to believe your story today when your life has been a lie?"

Cara's chest contracted as though every bit of oxygen was wrung from her lungs.

"Answer the question."

Cara opened her mouth, but words refused to squeeze past the constriction in her throat.

"All right, next question since you won't answer the first one. Did you have a child out of wedlock?" The bald counselor rocked back on his heels.

The assistant D.A. stood. "Objection. Relevance, Your Honor."

"Your Honor, this question and the ones to follow go to this witness's character. Mrs. Winters wants to portray herself as a moral, innocent woman attacked by these three young men and threatened by them in the parking lot." The defense attorney gestured toward his clients, seated at a table, in suits and ties, the picture of virtue.

Cara sucked in a breath but couldn't fill her lungs with enough air. Pain radiated through her. She glanced toward Noah. His features blank, cold, he sat stiffly, staring straight ahead, not at her.

"Overruled. Answer the question, Mrs. Winters."

The judge's kind expression didn't alleviate her panic bubbling to the surface. "Yes."

Some murmurs from the audience prompted the judge to bring his gavel down. "Quiet or I will clear the courtroom."

"Did your husband, whom you married in the hospital after giving birth, adopt your son?"

"Yes."

"So your husband wasn't the father of your child?"

"No."

"Who is?"

"Objection. Not relevant. Women have children out of wedlock all the time. The paternity of her child has nothing to do with the assault and battery charges."

"It will shortly become apparent, Your Honor."

The serious expression on the lawyer's thin face didn't bode well for Cara. How had he discovered what had happened nine years ago? Did he know everything? Her heart thudded a maddening pace that she was sure the jurors could hear.

"It better be or I'll cut it short. Overruled."

"Mrs. Winters, who is the father of your child?"

"I don't know."

More murmurs sounded. In the back row a young man, the same age as the defendants, exited the courtroom.

"Order in the courtroom," the judge bellowed. "Bailiff, escort the next person who causes a commotion out of here."

"Ah, so you had sex with a lot of men, so many you don't even know who your son's father really is. Is that right?"

Flushed with humiliation, Cara gripped her hands together in her lap so tightly that her knuckles whitened. "No!"

The lawyer's eyebrows rose. "I am prepared to present a witness who went to high school with you who will testify to what happened on prom night your senior year."

"Objection. Counsel is testifying."

"Sustained."

A slow smile curved the defense attorney's mouth. "Do you stand by your previous answer of no?"

"Yes."

"Then why don't you know who the father of your son is?"

She rubbed her clammy hands together and again tried to drag a decent breath into her lungs. "Because I was drunk and don't remember what happened." Renewed shame and guilt threatened the well-ordered life she had managed to create after that awful night.

"So you don't remember how many men you had *that* night. How about the other nights?"

Father, help me. Why this now? Haven't I been punished enough for this mistake?

"Would you please answer the question, Mrs. Winters?" The harsh lights in the courtroom glared off his bald head.

"I was a virgin when I went to that party, and other than my husband, I haven't been with anyone since prom night." Remembering her vow to herself and God never to do something like that again, she lifted her chin. "That's why I can answer no."

"You want the jury to believe that when you drink you conveniently forget what happens?"

"Your Honor, I object. This doesn't pertain to the assault and battery charges."

"I agree. Sustained. Move on, Counselor. I think we all get the picture."

"No more questions." Contempt infused the sentence as the defense attorney turned his back on Cara as though she was beneath his consideration.

She started to rise, her legs so weak and trembling she was afraid she would collapse before she made it to her seat. Although wounded and laid bare for the whole world to see, she wouldn't let the jury glimpse anything but honesty and conviction in her expression.

"I have one question on cross-examination." The assistant D.A. remained seated at his table. "Do you drink alcohol now?"

"No, I haven't since that night."

"Thank you, Mrs. Winters."

The smile he gave her brought tears to her eyes. She closed them briefly while composing herself.

"You may step down." The judge's words brought her back to the present.

She pushed to her feet, then descended from the witness box and crossed the courtroom floor. All eyes rested on her. She sensed hostility in many and sympathy in some. She couldn't look at Noah. She didn't want to know what he felt.

Her dark secret had been ripped from her soul. How would she ever explain that one night to the people she loved and cared about? She'd made a terrible mistake that she was still paying for. Years ago when she had come to Jesus, she had thrown herself on His mercy and asked for His forgiveness. She'd thought she had received it, but maybe she was wrong and this was her punishment.

Noah was called to testify. She waited for him to exit the row. Their gazes locked for a few seconds, then he headed toward the witness box. His unreadable look plunged her deeper into despair.

The sound of his voice, devoid of emotion, flowed over her as he gave his account of that night in the restaurant. How could he ever fall in love with her now? Tim had known what had happened at the party and the result of that one night of lost control. As her good friend he had married her for her son's sake, but even Tim couldn't in the end look past what she had done. In his eyes she had been damaged goods.

Her tears returned to sting her eyes. The second she swallowed the lump lodged in her throat, it rose again. She needed to leave Cimarron City and go someplace where she wouldn't be constantly reminded of what she could have had if she hadn't tried so hard in high school to fit in with the "cool" kids.

When the defense attorney approached Noah, Cara focused on Noah's testimony. Although there had been a few witnesses who had given evidence about the altercation among the three defendants and Cara and Noah in the restaurant, she and Noah were the main ones.

"Mr. Maxwell, you are quite familiar with fighting, especially as a way to solve your problems—" the lawyer paused "—aren't you?"

The man wasn't satisfied with destroying her. No, he was now going after Noah. His past troubles would be plastered all over the newspaper tomorrow alongside hers. He was a respected member of the community with a thriving business that she had already managed to damage. This could really hurt him, and she was the reason it was happening. She shouldn't have brought charges against Jake, Brent and Jeremy.

The suffocating air pressed in on her. She had to get out of there. As Noah answered the question, she bolted from the courtroom. The urge to keep running inundated her, but she settled herself on a bench outside in the corridor in an alcove away from prying eyes. She'd had her share of notoriety.

The silence in her car on the long ride home after the trial eroded Cara's shored-up defenses. The jury hadn't deliberated for long. The three young men had been found not guilty. Their cocky looks were imprinted on her mind forever. The celebration among their supporters and friends had started immediately and driven home whom the jury believed.

As she, Noah and Adam had left the courthouse, a mob of reporters had swamped them, wanting their statements. There had been no words to describe how she felt. Numb wasn't strong enough—in fact, it wasn't even close.

All she wanted to do was hold Timothy, then later cry until there were no more tears left. She didn't even have any energy to deal with Noah and the shock he must be experiencing after what he discovered about her in the courtroom today.

Why couldn't that part of her life stay in the past?

Noah drove through the opened gates and parked in his garage. Adam fled from the backseat the second Noah turned off the engine. Gripping the handle, Cara intended to leave and repair the damages to her emotions before talking to Noah.

"Last night when I was pouring my heart out to you, did you even think about telling me about Timothy?" Hurt made Noah's words even chillier.

"The time wasn't right," was all she could think of to say. She just wanted to escape, as fast as Adam had, and try to make sense of the situation before explaining anything to Noah or anyone else.

"When would the time have been right?" he whispered, his voice raw.

Her eyes filled with tears she didn't want to release in front of him. She thrust open the door and scrambled from the car. "I don't know." Then she hurried from the garage.

Wet tracks streamed down her face as she ran toward

the cottage. When she glanced back at the door into the guesthouse, she caught a glimpse of Noah on the deck. Darkness crept close as night approached. She was glad she couldn't see his expression. Today she'd seen enough people's low opinion of her in their faces.

Inside Laura sat on the couch reading a book. As Cara closed the door, her friend looked up. "I heard about the verdict. I'm so sorry."

Cara fluttered her hand in the air. "That's behind me. I'm not giving it any more of my time."

"Really?" Laura closed her paperback and laid it on the couch.

"Well, just as soon as I can get it behind me, I will keep it there. Is Timothy asleep already?"

"He played some this afternoon with Lindsay and Rusty when they came home from school, but it tired him out."

"Is he all right?" Cara strode toward her son's bedroom.

"He's fine. Remember he didn't get any sleep last night," Laura called from the living room.

Cara opened the door and peered in. He'd kicked the blanket off and one leg hung off the bed. She crossed to him and gently placed it upon the mattress, then brought the sheet up to cover him. She stood back and studied her son, trying to determine whom he looked like. Right after he was born, she'd done that a lot, but never could decide. Her parents had insisted he was the spitting image of her at that age.

Her son would never know his real dad and his adopted one was dead. She would have to be both mother and father for him now. Staring down at him, she knew what she had to do. She would give Noah her notice. She had to leave to protect not only herself, but mostly her son. How could she subject him to the ridicule the publicity would cause? Her whole sordid past was public knowledge.

Leaning over, she kissed him on the forehead, then tiptoed from the room. Some good could come out of bad. Timothy was proof of that.

Back in the living room she sat across from Laura in a chair. "I'm going to my parents. I may not stay long, but I can't stay here any longer. I'm giving Noah my notice. I hope he'll want us to leave as soon as possible."

"What about school?"

"Tomorrow is the last day. Hopefully no one will say anything to Timothy, and I know he'll want to tell all his friends goodbye."

"Why are you really running away?"

Cara frowned. "What do you mean? You heard what happened in the courtroom. In no time, everyone will have heard."

"Do you think you're the first person to have made a mistake?"

"No, but—"

"No one is perfect. Jesus was the only one who walked this earth who was perfect."

Cara shot to her feet. "I won't put my son through the snickering and name-calling. I won't—"

"You love Noah."

Cara paced across the room, then spun around, her hands clenched. "Yes. I did exactly what you warned me not to do. And you are right. Noah Maxwell doesn't fall in love. He doesn't want anyone in his life permanently."

"He told you that?"

"Let me put it this way, he has not confessed his

undying love for me. In fact, if you could have seen his face in court when he heard about Timothy, you would say he hates me."

"Has he told you that?"

"Well, no. Noah has more class than that. In the car coming back here, he managed to cover up his disgust with his usual unreadable expression." Cara finished her trek to the sink and turned on the cold tap water. "Do you want something to drink?"

"No, I need to go home, but you and I will talk again before you leave." Laura strode to her and hugged her. "You need to get a good night's sleep and then think about what you are going to do tomorrow. You should never make an important decision when you're exhausted."

Cara followed her friend to the door. As Laura left, Cara checked the deck. It was empty and the light was on in Noah's bedroom.

Why had she fallen in love with the impossible?

"Bye. Have fun the last day of school." On Noah's front porch, Cara waved to the children as they headed toward their bus stop.

Noah stood silent behind her. He'd said little through breakfast except when the kids asked him something. The moment was here. Before he left for work, she needed to tell him her decision to leave.

Swinging around, she inhaled a deep breath, prepared to launch into her spiel. He was gone. She hadn't even heard him open and close the door.

Quickly she moved into the house and found him in his study, gathering papers and stuffing them into a briefcase. She leaned against the jamb, hugging her arms to her. "I want to give my notice."

Noah paused in midaction. "Why?"

"I've decided to go to my parents for the summer. Timothy hasn't seen his grandparents in almost a year."

"So you're letting those guys run you out of town."

The steel behind his words cut through her. "It's for the best. I'll stay for a few weeks if you want, but I'd prefer to leave as soon as possible."

"What about Adam, Rusty and Lindsay?"

"I'll talk to them tonight and explain. If I stay, my past might affect them. I don't want to hurt them." She thought of the article on the front page of the newspaper this morning, detailing the events of the trial, and the fact that Noah had to take his phone off the hook to keep reporters from bothering them. Yes, the interest in her would eventually die down, but the damage would have been done.

"How am I supposed to find a housekeeper in such a short time?"

"Laura will help. There are several good agencies in town. The kids can stay with her during the day until you get a good one. Maybe a foster family will become available soon, then they will be out of your hair."

Noah flinched as if she had slapped him. "I thought you cared about what happened to them."

The barb punched her in the stomach. "I do, but I have to think of my son first."

"Have you told him about what was revealed at the trial?"

"Not yet. He was asleep when I got home last night and this morning he was slow getting ready for school. I will when he gets home."

"What if he hears about it at school?"

"I'm praying he doesn't."

"So after all that has happened, your faith is still strong?"

"Yes." Her belief was the only thing that had sustained her last night when she wanted to break down. She'd prayed to the Lord, trying to make sense out of the fact her mistake had resurfaced now. Then she remembered that, although God forgave us our sins, there were still consequences for our actions. *God is our refuge and strength, an ever-present help in trouble.* She would pull herself together and go on with His help.

A calm seeped into her until Noah broke the silence. "You come into my life and turn it upside down and just like that—" he snapped his fingers "—you walk away."

His harsh condemnation ripped through her, buckling her knees.

Chapter Thirteen

Noah's hands shook as he continued stuffing papers into his briefcase. "I appreciate you giving me notice, but by all means leave whenever you want. I'll call Laura and work something out."

Cara gripped the doorjamb. "I'm sorry about everything. I didn't mean for things to happen this way."

"Just make sure you tell the kids. They won't understand you suddenly being gone."

Because I don't. His own past loomed before him. He remembered his mother had been there when he'd gone to school in the morning and hadn't been when he'd come home. No goodbye. Nothing. Focusing on Whitney, who was only one when their mother left, was the only thing that had helped him get over his mom's abandonment—or so he had thought.

He was seven years old again, standing in the middle of the living room, holding a note from his mother that he couldn't read. He'd gone next door and had his neighbor tell him what it said. A myriad of emotions had bombarded him from anger to hurt to numbness. That was how he felt now.

He clutched his briefcase and headed toward the door, having to brush past Cara, so close her vanilla scent taunted him. Suddenly reminded of that time in the gazebo when he had kissed her, he nearly stumbled. Catching himself, he hurried from the house before he begged her to stay.

Better for her to be gone now than later. Before he fell—who was he kidding? He was in love with Cara. Probably had been for quite some time.

Noah slipped behind the steering wheel, stuck the key in the ignition but didn't turn the engine on. Staring out the windshield at the white wall of his garage, he couldn't believe after all these years carefully protecting himself from getting hurt again that he had given his heart away and she had crushed it.

Yesterday at the trial when he had discovered the truth about Timothy, at first he had been upset because he had wanted Cara to tell him. He had wanted her to trust him enough with the truth. The fact she hadn't had sucker punched him.

But last night as he'd read his Bible about forgiveness and judging others, he'd realized that Cara would have told him when she was ready if it hadn't been for the trial. He'd intended to talk to her after the children left for school, but she had dropped her bomb about leaving. What he had to say to her wasn't important anymore. If she didn't want to stay and help with the kids, see where their relationship would go, then he wanted to cut his losses now.

His gut twisted in a huge knot, Noah laid his forehead against the steering wheel. He had survived his mother and father leaving him; he would survive this, too. Somehow. *Lord, with Your help.*

* * *

I hate you, Mom. Why are we going away? I don't want to.

Timothy's words haunted Cara through the night. She rolled over in bed and punched her pillow. Over and over. But sleep evaded her.

Finally at six in the morning on Saturday she threw back the covers and got out of bed. She hadn't even gotten the chance to explain why Tim had adopted Timothy. Her son had run from the room and gone to Noah's house to see Rusty.

Well, today she intended to talk with her son and then the other children because she wanted to be on the road on Monday for Flagstaff.

Yesterday Noah hadn't come home until it was late and she was in the cottage. Part of her had been disappointed. Truthfully the less she saw of him, the better she would be. It was hard enough loving him and not having him return those feelings. Pain pierced through her heart as though it were cracking in half.

She shuffled to the closet and selected a pair of jeans and a T-shirt to wear. She'd never been in love before and that was part of the reason—actually most of the reason—her marriage to Tim had failed. He had loved her and she could never return it as he wanted her to. Yes, she cared for him. Yes, she thought of him as a good friend. But that hadn't been enough to hold their fragile marriage together. Slowly over the years Tim had grown to resent her lack of love even though he had insisted he didn't care when they had married for Timothy's sake.

After donning her clothes, she went across the hall to check on her son. When she opened his door and spied his empty bed, panic took root. She went through the cottage and discovered it was as empty as the bed.

Trembling, fear mingling with panic, she hurried toward the main house. He probably got up early and had made plans with Rusty to play, get in as much as they could before they left for her parents'.

But when she entered Noah's place, quiet greeted her as if everyone was still asleep. She took the stairs two at a time and eased Rusty's bedroom door open. His bed was empty, too. Her panic burgeoned. Not again. Had they all run away?

She quickly checked Lindsay's and Adam's rooms and found them still sleeping. Rushing down the steps to the first floor, intending to search every room, she collided with Noah coming out of the kitchen, his hair tousled, a day's growth of beard on his face, an exhausted look in his eyes as if he had been up most of the night, too.

As he steadied her, surprise flittered across his features until they settled into that impenetrable expression she'd seen too much lately. "Why are you here so early?" His gaze drilled into her. "What's wrong? Did Timothy have another asthma attack?"

She shook her head, aware Noah's hands still grasped her arms. "Timothy and Rusty aren't in their rooms. I can't find my son!"

Everything came crashing down around her. Nothing was working the way she had planned. He studied her for a few seconds, his countenance taking on an emotion: concern. Dragging her against him, he embraced her.

"They're probably someplace around here. We'll take a look. It's not easy for them to get off the property and no one has opened the gate."

The calm in his voice soothed her panic until she remembered how angry Timothy had been with her last night. "He was so upset when I told him about leaving and that Tim wasn't his real father but had adopted him. I've never seen him like that. All I wanted to do was protect him."

"From what?"

"From all that has happened recently. From the kind of people who protested for those ballplayers. From being hurt any more because of what I did. And all of that was for nothing. The men got off scot-free." Cara looked up into Noah's face.

"You didn't see the news last night?"

"No."

"A young college woman has come forward to file charges against Jake, Brent and Jeremy. According to her, they actually did to her what they would have done to you if they had gotten you into their car."

"Why didn't she say anything earlier?"

"She was afraid, but after seeing what happened to you, she's decided they need to pay for what they have done. Let's find the kids then we'll talk some more. Okay?"

She nodded, a ray of hope bursting through the gloom shrouding her. "I'll take this half of the house and the garage, too."

After Cara searched the living, dining and utility rooms, she went out into the garage and came to a halt a few feet from the door. A white SUV was parked in the space where Noah's sports car had always sat. Seeing the new vehicle confirmed in her mind that Adam, Rusty and Lindsay would be all right once she left. Noah made a commitment to be their foster parent even after knowing she was leaving.

She quickly skirted the SUV, checked the three-car garage, and then met Noah in the kitchen. "Nothing."

"I didn't find anything, either. Let's take a look outside. You can look around the pool and the cabana while I check the gazebo and pond area and the tree house."

"It's not finished."

"That might be the lure for two boys."

Again Cara found neither Timothy nor Rusty. Her optimism dimmed as she made her way toward the tree fort. Noah climbed the wooden ladder that led to the multileveled platforms, the only part constructed.

Noah peered over the side of the highest flooring. "They're up here."

From the ground Cara couldn't see anyone. She hurried toward the coral tree's trunk. "I'm coming up."

Not particularly fond of heights, she carefully ascended into the top of the branches. Timothy and Rusty sat cross-legged on the planks, a mutinous expression on their faces, blankets and pillows behind them. She crawled toward the center, trying not to think how far up she was.

"How long have you two been up here?" she asked, kneeling next to Noah.

Timothy jutted his chin out. "All night."

"All night! You climbed up here in the dark?"

Rusty held up a flashlight. "We used this."

"We slept up here, Mom."

"What if you had rolled off during the night? Did you two think about that?"

Timothy and Rusty stared at each other, the fact they hadn't considered that dawning on their faces. Their eyes grew round. Rusty eased over to the side and looked down, then whistled.

"Timothy, you go back to the cottage. You and I will talk in a minute."

Her son squared his shoulders, his frown back in place. "I don't want to leave. I like it here. I don't care what happened at the trial. I don't care that Dad wasn't my real father."

"How do you know about what happened at the trial?"

"I asked Adam. He told me."

A wave of hurt crashed into her. She had been the one who had wanted to explain about what was said at the trial, but her son had preferred hearing it from Adam. She still needed to explain, and she didn't want to have this discussion twenty feet off the ground with Noah and Rusty looking on. "Go back to the cottage now. We're gonna finish our talk from last night. And when I get down, you better be there. No more running away."

"Rusty, you, too." Noah moved to the side so the boys could crawl past them.

Reluctantly the two left. After their departure, Cara glanced toward Noah to thank him for helping her. The words died on her tongue. The caring look he gave her wiped everything from her mind—even the fact she was in the top of a large tree. All she could focus on was the love in his eyes.

He tried to shift away to hide his expression. Cara caught his arm and stopped him. Hope flamed bright.

"Why were you so upset at the trial while I was testifying?" she asked, her question barely sounding around the love jamming her throat.

Pain tangled with the love she saw on his face. "I couldn't protect you from what the defense attorney was trying to do to you. He was trying to destroy your reputation and all I could do was sit and watch while he did. I felt so helpless."

She inched closer, lifting her hand to touch his firm jaw, a nerve twitching. "That's what I felt while I listened to your testimony."

"I've been thinking about what you said about that night at the party. How much did you have to drink?"

She thought back to the party and tried to count how many. She couldn't get past three. "Three drinks and I don't even think I took more than a few sips of the third one. That's all I remember, then everything is a blank until I woke up."

"I wonder if someone slipped some drug like Rufie into your drink."

Stunned, Cara sank back against the tree trunk. "I just assumed I couldn't handle alcohol. That was my first and last time drinking. And I was so ashamed by my behavior that I didn't consider anything beyond that. All I wanted to do was get home and lick my wounds. It wasn't until much later that I realized the full scope of what happened at the party."

"Why were you ashamed? Because you made a mistake? Everyone makes them." He closed the space between them.

"That's what Laura told me, but what I did was wrong and I'm still facing the consequences of that action. Truthfully I never wanted my son to know the circumstances of how he was conceived."

"So you didn't plan to ever to tell him that he was adopted?"

"Tim insisted on it and I agreed to it. Tim wanted to be Timothy's only father. He didn't want his son wondering who his real dad was."

"This past few months with the children has led me to believe the biological father isn't what is really important.

It's the person who is there for the kids on a day-to-day basis, supporting them, loving them, disciplining them with a caring hand. Mine never was there, but Paul was." He cocked a grin. "And now I know why Paul took all those children in. I've gained more from this arrangement than Adam, Rusty or Lindsay have."

"More than that white SUV sitting in your garage?"

His smile grew. "I was getting tired of having to borrow your car to transport the children."

"I didn't see your Corvette. Where is it?"

"At the dealership waiting to be sold." Noah ran his finger up her arm.

"You traded it in," she said in a breathless voice, his touch producing a sharp awareness of him. "I thought you said something about getting an SUV in addition to the sports car."

"Those days are behind me. I want to be the children's foster parent on a permanent basis. I called the case manager up and told her to stop looking for a family to take them in."

"When?"

"Thursday morning before we left for the trial. I was going to tell you afterward. But the time never seemed right."

She had to take the risk. "I love you, Noah."

"Then why did you want to leave me?"

"Because I couldn't stay here and be around you when you didn't love me. As much as I care for the children, I can't do it."

A smile lit his face. "So if I love you with all my heart, you will stay—" he slid his hands into her hair "—and marry me?"

"Are you proposing to me?"

"Yes." He brought her to him, his mouth covering hers in a deep, soul-searching kiss. "I want to spend the rest of my life with you. You have shown me how faith and family can make a man rich beyond any monetary amount. I want to continue to explore both with you by my side. Cara Winters, will you marry me?"

"Hmm. I may have to think about that."

"Good thing this isn't a limited time offer."

She laughed. "Well, I guess I'll put you out of your misery." She threw her arms around his neck and kissed him. "Yes, I'll marry you for all the right reasons. Love."

"I don't want to wait long. How's next month sound to you?"

"My, you move fast."

"I'm almost thirty-six years old. I'd say I've moved slow." Taking her hand, he laced his fingers through hers. "How do you think the kids will take the news about our marriage?"

"Hmm. Let me see. Are we talking about the same children who tried to get us together with that dinner?"

"I want to adopt them, including your son. Do you think they will agree?"

"I don't know. The best way to find out is to ask them."

He tugged on her hand. "Then let's go together and talk to all of them about us being a family."

Epilogue

"Can I have everyone's attention?" Noah stood in the middle of his great room with Cara next to him. Draping an arm over her shoulder, he pulled her close as their crowd of friends quieted. "I have an announcement."

"We already know Cara is pregnant and those ballplayers finally got what they deserved," Peter shouted from the back. "That's old news."

Laura playfully punched her husband in the arm. "We just found out yesterday. That's not old news."

Timothy ran into the room with Rusty and Molly following him. Both boys came to a skidding halt in front of Noah. Huge grins welcomed him when he looked down at them. Somehow they knew he had wanted it to be a surprise.

"Okay. Enough stalling." Jacob took Hannah's hand. "I, for one, am hungry, but if you don't quit being so dramatic, I'll never have my say at the dinner table."

A couple of the children giggled. Adam and Sean began to talk.

Alice brought her cane down on the hardwood floor. "Silence. Let's give Noah a chance to tell us."

"Yesterday afternoon I got the news that Cara and I will be allowed to adopt Adam, Rusty and Lindsay. We'll be going to court next week to start the process." And soon after that he would appear in court to finalize his adoption of Timothy.

Cheers broke out in the room.

Lindsay approached Cara and hugged her around the waist. "Does this mean we're a family now?"

Cara smoothed the girl's hair back from her face. "Honey, we've always been a family. This will just make it official."

"Okay, let's eat," Jacob called out near the kitchen.

"You would think he was pregnant the way he thinks about food," Noah muttered to Cara, then kissed her on the mouth.

As the crowd filed into the dining room, Cara stopped Noah. "Are you okay?"

He dragged her to him and framed her face. "You know me so well. I called Whitney this morning to wish her a happy Thanksgiving and the phone has been disconnected."

"Oh, Noah, I'm sorry. Are you going to have the P.I. try and find her again?"

"I don't know. I thought she was finally accepting me back in her life, but I guess I was wrong. I'd even asked her to come for Christmas, and I thought she was really considering it."

"C'mon, you two lovebirds. We can't eat without the host and hostess," Jacob said from the entrance into the dining room.

Noah started forward. The doorbell sounded above the noise. "Everyone is here, aren't they?"

"Maybe Lisa changed her mind and decided to have Thanksgiving dinner with the boss after all." Cara altered her direction and moved toward the foyer.

"You go sit down. I'll get this." Noah redirected her toward the dining room, then crossed the entryway to open the front door.

Standing on the porch was his sister with a black eye and a cast on her left arm. Shock whisked all words from his mind.

"Aren't you going to ask me in?" Wariness and a bit of defiance marked her expression.

"What happened?"

"My latest boyfriend was showing his appreciation so I hightailed it out of there."

Noah noticed several pieces of luggage behind Whitney. "Are you taking me up on my offer to move to Cimarron City? I have a guesthouse just waiting for a guest to stay in it."

She nodded, tension in every line of her body. "Just until I get back on my feet and only if you let me carry my own weight around here. Otherwise, I'm out of here."

He would take any amount of time with his baby sister. "Fine. I can live with that."

Someone yelled from the dining room for him to come eat before the food got cold.

Whitney looked around him into the house. "If you just point me in the direction of the guesthouse, you can get back to whatever you were doing."

"No."

She blinked and stepped back. "Well, then—"

"I want you to come in and have Thanksgiving dinner with my family and friends."

She shook her head, taking another pace back. "I don't be—"

Noah crossed the gap between them. "You are part of my family. Please come in and meet everyone."

She waved her hand down her body, indicating her jeans with holes in them and her old jacket with a rip in the pocket. "I'm not dressed to meet them."

"Your appearance has capped off a great day. Please share it with me." He held out his hand to her.

She stared at it for a long moment, shrugged and fit hers in his grasp. "What about my suitcases?"

"I'll come back and bring them inside after I introduce you to everyone and give thanks to the Lord for such a special blessing."

When Noah entered the dining room with his sister by his side, his family and friends suddenly stopped talking. He caught Cara's gaze, and the smile that graced her mouth conveyed her love and support. With Cara and Jesus in his live, anything was possible, even the mending of his rift with his sister.

* * * * *

In October, be sure to read Margaret Daley's
FORSAKEN CANYON,
available from Love Inspired Suspense.
And in 2009, look for Whitney's story
in Love Inspired.

Dear Reader,

This is the third story in my FOSTERED BY LOVE miniseries. Noah is thrown into a situation for which he isn't prepared. Reluctantly, he becomes a foster parent and immediately realizes he is in over his head. Thankfully, he has Cara to turn to for help. Being a parent is one of the most important jobs we can ever have. And yet, it is one of the hardest jobs. This story is a tribute to all parents.

Whitney, Noah's sister, will get her chance at love in the next FOSTERED BY LOVE installment. Be sure to look for her story in 2009.

I love hearing from readers. You can contact me at P.O. Box 2074, Tulsa, OK 74101, or visit my Web site at www.margaretdaley.com where you can sign up for my quarterly newsletter.

May God bless you,

Margaret Daley

QUESTIONS FOR DISCUSSION

1. Noah felt he let down his sister when he couldn't protect her from their father. Have you ever felt as though you've disappointed someone? What has helped you get through it?

2. Cara made a mistake when she was a teenager that she is still paying for. Although the Lord has forgiven her, she still has to face the consequences of her actions. When have you made a mistake and had to deal with the consequences? How did you seek forgiveness?

3. Because he knew what it was like to be separated from his sibling, Noah was determined to keep Adam's family together. In order to do that, he had to step forward and do something he felt unequipped to handle—be a parent. What experiences have you been forced to handle when you didn't have the right expertise? Who or what did you rely on for help?

4. Who was your favorite character? What about this character appealed to you?

5. Shame is a powerful emotion. Cara couldn't get over the shame of what she had done as a teenager. It was what drove her away from Noah. How can your faith help you through feeling ashamed?

6. *Family Ever After* is partly a story of abandonment. Noah was abandoned by his mother and father.

Adam, Rusty and Lindsay were abandoned by their father. How does a person work her way through the feelings generated when a loved one abandons her? How can the Lord help? What Bible verses can a person read to help cope with the situation?

7. What is your favorite scene in the book? Why?

8. Cara helps Noah discover the importance of the Lord in his life. Have you helped someone find his way to the Lord? How did you do it?

9. People in the town judged Cara. I used the verse from John. "If any one of you is without sin, let him be the first to throw a stone at her." We often find ourselves judging someone, sometimes unjustly. How can we avoid doing that? Are there other verses to help us with judging people?

10. Noah thought if he could avoid having a committed relationship, he wouldn't be hurt or disappointed. He never wanted to risk his heart again…but life *is* full of risks. What risks have you taken? Were the risks worth the rewards?

11. It was important for Noah to remain in control of his life. As a child, he'd felt as if his life was out of his control. When have you felt your life was like that? Have you turned to the Lord and given control over to Him? What Bible verses help you deal with this situation?

12. I picked the verse from Psalm 37:39 ("But the salvation of the righteous is of the Lord: He is their

strength in the time of trouble.") as the one at the beginning of *Family Ever After.* Why do you think I chose that verse? Is the Lord the first one you turn to when you have a problem? What does finding strength in the Lord during troubled times have to do with this story?